Color Blind

I0618973

COLOR BLIND

RYAN J. PELTON

Rock House Publishing
Kansas City

Color Blind

An Antique Assassin Crime Novel

Book 3

This is a work of fiction. All of the characters, organizations, locations, and events portrayed in this novel are either product's of the author's imagination or are used fictitiously.

Second Edition

ISBN 13: 978-1-949420-06-7

Published, formatted, and designed by Rock House Publishing www.rockhousepublishing.com

For latest releases and updates visit ryanjpelton.com/fiction

Other Books by Author

Antique Assassin Crime Adventure series
Hired Gun (Book 1)
Stranger Danger (Book 2)
First Blood (Book 4-prequel)
Stand Alone Novels
The Boardwalk
Shorts
Watched
The Ricky Rayburn Chronicles
Middle Grade Fiction (8-12)
Secrets of the Ambassadors
Mysterious Pirates of the Pacific (Fall 2018)
Book 3 (Winter 2018)

Darkness cannot drive out darkness; only light can do that. Hate cannot drive out hate; only love can do that.
Martin Luther King Jr.

1.

Nelson Darby held his arm steady, staring down the long black barrel. A car rushed in front of his eyes and he backed off to reset.

Really?

He sighed, steadied himself, and turned his baseball cap around, while snapping a lucky piece of gum. Trident.

The double lane street was busy with the normal lunchtime traffic in downtown LeClaire, Missouri. The restaurants were filled with a mixture of day laborers and white and blue collar workers, white, black, young and old.

Nelson locked in on a handsome African American couple sipping Iced Tea and gazing deep into each other's eyes. Married? Dating? Brother and sister? Who knows?

He twisted the barrel slightly to the right and back to the left. Squinting his eye, he took one last breath before pulling the trigger.

Click.

He pulled the Canon SLR1 back and examined the small LCD screen. Nelson pressed a button on top of the camera and waited for it to change.

Looked like a winner.

Nelson unscrewed the long lens and packed it in a black carrying case. He edged to the curb, checked both ways for traffic, spit out the gum, and galloped across the street.

The young black couple, of about twenty, with faces immersed in salads, sandwiches, and each other, were oblivious to the scrawny white man standing at the edge of their table.

Nelson stuck out a hand, "Sorry to bother you in the middle of lunch. Do you have a second?" he asked, adjusting the camera bag wrapped around his shoulder.

A strong, wide-chested man peeked up from his salad, annoyed by the interruption. His good look-ing companion, sitting across the round patio table, squirmed in her seat, wiped the remnants of a Turkey Club from her lip, and gripped his hand across the table.

"We're trying to eat lunch. What's this about?" the man asked.

Nelson's hand dangled over the middle of the table; he pulled it back, and continued his spiel, "Name's Nelson and I'm a photography student at LeClaire Community College. Been photograph-ing an eagle perched above the top of the restaurant and you beautiful people caught my eye," Nelson said, pointing to a Maple tree hovering over the sign: All Seasons Cafe.

The black man raised a brow and glanced at the woman. "Okay... what do you want?"

"Well, I, ugh, took a couple pics of you eating lunch. That okay?" Nelson asked, as he jammed his hands into his jean pockets, trying to keep the camera bag steady on his shoulder.

"Why are you taking pictures of us? Never seen black folks in LeClaire before? Rare as that eagle you were photographing," the man said with a grin, looking for confirmation from his girlfriend.

Nelson gave an awkward half-smile as his face turned red. He shuffled his Converse on the hot cement, "You're black? Didn't notice. My momma taught us to be colorblind. Wasn't it Martin Luther King who said it's not the color of the skin, but...."

The man held up a hand. "Stop before you embarrass yourself. Got it. You're not a racist," he said, taking a sip of Iced Tea.

Nelson swung his camera bag off his shoulder and flipped open a large compartment in the top. He yanked out a small business card and handed one to the couple. A car honked behind him causing him to lurch.

"Like I said, I was trying to shoot a rare eagle in Missouri. Never seen one in the city..."

The man examined the card and looked back at Nelson. "How does this concern us?" he asked.

"I'm looking for models to help with a website design and marketing project for class. You're a beautiful couple and just what I need. Interested?" Nelson asked with a toothy grin.

The black man cleared his throat, "I'm guessing you need a token black couple for the project. Appear inclusive and diverse. Is that what this is all about?" he asked, watching as his girlfriend shook her head.

"Oh no, sir. I think you two have impeccable features and could make serious money with your flawless faces. And, help a starving artist," Nelson said, closing the camera bag.

The woman examined the card and smiled. "You think we have impeccable features? Few famous models come out of LeClaire," she said.

"Few famous people period. I think the most famous was the guy who won American Idol, David something," Nelson said.

They both laughed.

"This sounds fishy. But, what if we were interested? Is there an audition or something?" the man asked, wiping a bead of sweat from his perfect complexion.

Nelson leaned over the table and pointed at the business card. "No audition. Seen everything I need. All you need to do is visit the website, key in the password, and you'll see some of my past work. If you think this is something that might interest you, call the number at the bottom. I'll take care of the rest," he said as he stepped away from the table and dodged a man riding a bike down the sidewalk.

The couple looked at one another and then back at Nelson.

Nelson said, "No pressure. Not every day you run into such beautiful people. I want to capture this moment. I think we could be on to something good for everyone."

The woman batted her long eyelashes and placed her hand on her boyfriend. "Come on honey. Let's check out the website. What's the harm?" she asked.

He examined the card and then glanced up at Nelson. "All right. We'll check it out. Can we please finish the rest of our lunch?" he asked, peeking at a wristwatch.

Nelson held up his hands in supplication. "Thanks for allowing me to interrupt your lunch. You will not regret checking out the website. I think you'll like my work. Maybe you'll be the next famous people from LeClaire. Like the American Idol guy..."

The couple looked at each other and smiled.

Nelson glided back across the street and unlocked the door to an older Honda Civic. He fiddled with his camera bag, pulled out the Canon, and rolled down the window. He aimed it through the opening.

One more photo of these beautiful people. A people that deserved to be wiped from the earth.

2.

Dexter O'Kane tapped on a keyboard, scratched his head, and stared into the glow of a 24-inch computer monitor. Antique Adventures was quiet as the store did not open for another hour. John Wood exploded through the front doors.

"Are you kidding me?" he asked, waving a yellow paper in the air.

"What's that? DNA test proving you were raised by wolves?"

He leaned on the glass counter in the back of the store and caught his breath. "Funny, jerk. Got a ticket. Said I needed a front license plate on my car. Are LPD that bored?"

Dexter nodded, knowing crime in LeClaire wasn't comparable to LA or Kansas City. Even if you included the psychopathic serial killer they had taken down a couple years back or the Italian crime family last year. LeClaire mostly not a haven of evil.

"I hear you big fella. Got a ticket for rolling through a stop sign on Grant Street. Said I was a danger to society," Dexter said, not lifting his gaze from the computer screen.

John jammed the ticket into his pocket and came around to the computer Dexter was poking at. He pointed at the screen populated with websites. "You looking at porn?" he asked, breathing heavy.

"Only you do that. I'm happily married. We need an online presence. Our website is from the dark ages. E-commerce is how we can reach the world with our rusty gold," Dexter said.

Antique Adventures had always been a word-of-mouth business. Dexter and John drove the back-woods and highways and byways to find rusty gold, antiques for the laymen. You didn't need a fancy website to reach customers in the past. They were the only antique shop in LeClaire and had done well. But, times were changing. With HGTV, every hipster and yuppy in America wanted cool antiques to adorn their suburban homes. Good for AA, but the lack of a viable website would hurt business if not addressed.

"How are we going to find someone to build a site? I'm all for better technology but I don't need another role on my job description. As Vice President of the company, I can't update a website among all the other stuff going on."

Dexter smirked knowing single John had little going on, other than helping Dexter find antiques, playing video games, building new technology for the side business, and drinking Cherry Cokes. He had time. "Don't worry VP. I won't make you do it. Busy these days?"

"Well, yeah. Between building technology for the side gig, ugh, staying updated on the latest video games, and drinks at O'Malley's, who has time for website maintenance? Not to mention prowling for women on the internet."

"The fact you use the word prowling is why you're single. Women don't want prowlers.

John stuck out his tongue.

"I'm looking for someone to do it for us. I wouldn't want to impede your video games and prowling," Dexter said, with a wink.

Dexter scrolled a couple more sites and stopped at one, "This one looks interesting. Local kid. Nelson Darby Photography. Does web design and maintenance. Student at LeClaire Community College."

John scratched his head and gave a ruffled face like he didn't like the choice, "You're the President. But, hiring a college kid might be risky. We want to grow the business. I don't know if he could take our online presence to another level. Besides, he most likely plays video games all day and is irresponsible. Kids these days..." John said, shaking his head.

"You'd get along great. But, good point. I guess we need to consider cost versus experience. There are plenty of design firms that'll charge an arm and a leg. I don't want to break the bank. We're still making money with a website from the 90's. Maybe give him a chance? Save a buck. What do you think?"

John paused and adjusted his sloppy workout pants that were displaying his butt crack, "We need a professional. Keep looking. Let's find someone middle of the road. Not too expensive, maybe some experience, out of college."

Dexter nodded, not surprised with John's response. John was the play it safe guy and Dexter was the cowboy. He had started Antique Adventures with a hundred bucks, his life's savings, and hadn't cared if it took off. Collecting rusty gold's been his passion since youth and he wanted to see it work. Paid for what he loved. He now supports a family and two full time employees. Not bad for a hundred dollar investment.

AA was not entirely a success story. A few years back, in the midst of Dexter's first family being killed in a car accident, the business was on life support. If not for the side business, he might have had to look for work at the electrical plant in Harrisonville.

"Yeah, we need professionals on the team," Dexter said, glaring at John's butt crack, "I'll keep looking and set up a few interviews. Sound okay?"

John ignored the comment and moved a lamp sitting on a high shelf behind Dexter. He glanced down, "You say something?"

"I decided you will build the website. We can save money that way."

John stepped down from the step-ladder and stood akimbo, "What? Dex, I don't have time for that."

"You weren't listening, as usual. I'll bring people in for interviews, cool?"

"Oh... okay. I have an important meeting this week, anyway."

"Online Halo game?"

John swayed side to side and chewed on his index finger, "Maybe. The new version just came out. It means a lot. The dating scene is not good, of late."

Dexter raised his hands from the computer, "No judgment. I'll just talk behind your back later. Maybe ease up on the prowling and see how that works," Dexter said, slapping John's flabby arm.

Dexter left the computer and sauntered to the front of the store. He flipped over the Open sign and unlocked the glass door. "Our website might suck. But, at least people still buy stuff in person."

3.

Ray Carter and Elizabeth Waters held hands as they strolled down Main Street in LeClaire. They had dated since freshmen year and now graduation from Missouri University loomed ahead, in two months.

The proposal had gone as Ray envisioned. He had taken Elizabeth down to their first dating site, near the Missouri River, where they had a picnic. He expressed his love, opened the picnic basket, and the ring swam in a glass of Champagne. Elizabeth knew it was coming, but the wait was longer than expected.

"You believe that guy at lunch? Do you think he is a photographer looking for models? He kind of creeped me out," Ray said.

Elizabeth swung their clasped hands up and down with a child-like grin, "Maybe he's legit and wants to see us become famous. We do have impeccable features, ya know?" she said, winking at Ray.

"Even if this guy is needing help on a project. We don't have time with graduation in a few months and a wedding to plan later this summer. He creeps me out, babe," he said.

"Yes, a wedding. I like the sound of that. I can't wait to be Mrs. Carter," she said, leaning in for a kiss.

Ray finished the kiss and held the business card up in the air. The Missouri sun reflected off the silver writing around the letters of the name: Nelson Darby Photography.

"I can't trust a dude named Nelson. It sounds fishy," he said, with a laugh.

Elizabeth ripped the card back from Ray and examined it. They continued to walk and arrived in front of her apartment. "Let's check out the website. If it's weird, no harm, no foul, we ignore the man. If it looks legit, we call him. Sound good?" she asked.

Ray nodded, and they climbed the large cement steps to a set of brown double doors. Elizabeth punched in a code on a keypad and the door clicked open. They wound up three flights of stairs and unlocked the door to her apartment.

The door squeaked open and sunlight burst through the large window overlooking downtown LeClaire. A mixture of potpourri punched them in the face. "Did a Missouri meadow die in here? I need to use the bathroom," Ray said, airing out his nose.

Elizabeth punched him in the arm, "Smells better than sweaty gym socks like your apartment. You know where the bathroom is... loser," Elizabeth said, powering on her laptop.

Ray disappeared into a back hallway and Elizabeth typed in the web address from the card Nelson had given them. She spoke the letters off the card as she typed in the web browser: www.nelson-darbyphotography.com.

She waited for it to load. The website forwarded to another site: www.supremebeings.com, "Interesting name for a photography website. Maybe the 'supreme' stands for all the beautiful models of the world, like me," Elizabeth said, flipping her dark hair.

The website populated the screen. A black password box appeared in the center. Elizabeth scratched her long brown hair, flipped over the card, and typed in the password: fascinating people.

"Strange password," Elizabeth mumbled.

Ray strolled back into the room, wiped his wet hands on his black jeans, and stared over Elizabeth's shoulder as the website loaded. "What ya doing?"

"Checking out Nelson's site. It should be up soon."

"You want to be America's Next Top Model,

don't you? Elizabeth Waters, queen of LeClaire," he said, kissing her neck.

She giggled.

"Remember, you're my queen. If you become a famous model, don't forget your future husband," he said.

"I like the sound of that... future husband," she said.

Images buffered and populated on the computer screen. The blurry images cleared and multiple faces emerged on the screen. They leaned closer to the fifteen inch laptop screen.

A Hispanic woman pushing a small child in a swing. An Indian man eating an ice cream cone at a bus stop. A small Asian girl skipping rope with a group of other children. Two police officers standing over a young black man with hands cuffed behind his back. A young black couple eating lunch on a patio in front of a restaurant.

Elizabeth pointed at the screen, "Baby, there we are. Nelson was right. We are a beautiful couple," she said, staring up at Ray.

"Yeah, we're good looking if I do say so myself," he said.

"You notice something?" she asked, scrolling up and down the website, "All the pictures are ethnic minorities," Elizabeth said.

"Thought the same thing. You see, the dude in cuffs with the police aiming guns at him? What's that about?" Ray asked.

"Maybe he wants to diversify his portfolio with some colored folks? What do you think? Should we call him? He takes nice pictures. And, I love the diversity."

"It seems off. Besides, the wedding, graduation, we have a lot going on. Do we have time for modeling?"

The couple both stared at the screen as the images faded. A pop up window came into view with a message.

Glad you found my pictures. I wanted to highlight my fascination with these groups of people. A swath of the population I consider inferior, lesser, and not worthy to breathe the air of the supreme race, white people. The pure breed. The ones who make America a special place. Much of the country is being crowded out by people of color, and that must stop. It will stop, I promise. These lesser beings are a drain on the political, economic, and religious landscape of this fine country.

For now, I live with the fascination of how ugly these people are. I will continue to capture their images as monuments for a day when they no longer exist. At least in LeClaire. Have a nice day. Nelson Darby Photography.

Elizabeth and Ray sat with mouths and eyes wide open.

Silence.

Elizabeth gently closed the laptop, and a tear ran down her face. Ray placed his head in his hands and shook it side to side.

Ray raised his head and caressed Elizabeth's back, "I thought our country was getting better. Maybe not, when guys like Nelson Darby are doing this kind of nonsense. I think we know our answer..."

4.

Nelson Darby pushed on the bedroom door, tossed his camera bag on his dated Star Wars sheets, and loosened his baggy jeans. The smell of the room was a mix of incense and body odor.

He yanked off his Converse and T-shirt, and stood over the bed in his boxer shorts. Nelson followed behind the camera bag and plopped on the bed, gave a sigh, clasped his fingers behind his head, and stared at the ceiling.

A Confederate flag was draped across the ceiling, tacked up with four small knives. He examined the flag for a beat and then looked over at the camera bag laying on the left side of the bed. Nelson opened the top compartment of the bag, powered on the camera, and flipped on the LCD screen.

He scrolled through the pictures and smiled.

Look at the dregs of society. Yet, they're so dark and unique. The way the hair is so unlike the white man. Before long, wiped from the earth.

Nelson powered down the camera, opened the side compartment, and yanked out the memory card. He walked to a wooden computer desk in the corner of the dimly lit bedroom. He fired on the computer and waited for it to come alive. Nelson jammed the card in the computer tower sitting under the desk.

A group of Hispanic couples populated the screen. He clicked a couple times on his mouse and scrolled through the hundreds of pictures on the screen. The photo editing software filled with ethnic minorities from young to old. He scrolled faster and his smile grew bigger.

Fascinating. Look at that one. He's the largest man I've ever seen. Like a monster. No wonder these people can never find jobs. Wow... that guy looks straight up dumb. Probably can't count to three. How do these people function in society? What a drain...

Nelson paused on the picture of Ray and Elizabeth. They might be black. But, they are handsome. "I wonder if they'll check out my site," he said with a laugh.

He downloaded all the pictures to the computer hard drive and shut it off. Nelson glided over to a CD player on the opposite side of the room. A stack of CDs rose against the wall on a plastic rack. He thumbed through a couple titles, mostly heavy metal, and yanked one from the jewel case. He held it under the dim light of a desk lamp to check for scratches.

Feels like an AC/DC kind of night.

Nelson placed the CD in the top compartment and cranked up the volume as Thunderstruck blared through the speakers on the floor. He gave a couple head bangs, raised devil horns with his fingers, plopped back on the bed, and reached over to a magazine on the bedside table.

A guitar solo began, and he banged his head up and down on the pillow. Nelson flipped through the pages of the magazine, examining each page with a close eye. He mouthed the words as he read each article, like it was Holy writ.

My Bible. Every issue of American Renaissance gets better and better. It'll be a great day when enlightened people realize race and politics matter. I don't care what our left wing nut jobs think. These people need to be stopped. Jarrett Stevens is a genius. His message must meet the masses. I would love to meet him someday, he thought.

Nelson finished the magazine as the AC/DC album ended on the CD player. He tossed the magazine on the end table and nodded off to sleep. The whites of his eyes fluttered, and he was just about asleep when his cell phone buzzed with excitement. Nelson leaned over and shook off his sleepy head to see the number.

He swiped it on, "This is Nelson."

A young woman with a Spanish accent spoke

up. "Yes, hello, Nelson. This is Juanita Torres. I was wondering if our pictures were ready on the website?" she asked.

"Why yes, Juanita? I downloaded them this evening. They came out beautifully. I hope you're pleased with my work. Remember, type in the password on the website for instant access. If you have any problems, call me back," Nelson said, trying to hold back a smile.

"Thank you very much Mr. Darby. I'm looking forward to working with you. Like you said, I hope to be the next Jennifer Lopez," she said.

"You're a beauty. Going to be a star Juanita, I know it," Nelson said, mouthing the word no.

She hung up the phone.

Nelson raised his hands over his head and stared at the Confederate flag. He smiled and closed his eyes.

Another satisfied customer.

5.

The smell of fried eggs and bacon wafted through the sunlit living room. Morning came early as Nelson had spent a restless night thinking about the photographs from the day before. Something unsettled him.

Nelson scratched his crotch, rubbed his eyes, and stood at the entry of the living room. His mother, wearing a pink robe and white bathroom slippers, flipped channels in a leather Lazy Boy.

"You believe this crap. The Mexicans are taking all the jobs and killing our children," she said, sipping a Bloody Mary from a mason jar.

Nelson ignored his ranting mother and slid into the kitchen, following the delicious aroma.

"What's your mother bitching about?" asked his dad.

"Mexicans stealing our children. I wasn't really listening. She's drinking again."

His father flipped an egg and slid a pound of

bacon on a plate from a second pan, "She can have one Bloody Mary on Saturday's," he said, scratching his man-breasts under his stained ribbed tank top.

"Glad to see A.A. is working," Nelson said.

No response.

"Your mother's right about the Mexicans. These brown people are coming into my country and making a mess of things. Taking our jobs and killing our kids. Our neighbor, Joe, the plumber can't find work because Mexicans do it cheaper. They need to be stopped," he said, tearing off a piece of bacon between his crooked and darkened teeth.

Nelson scrunched his face watching his father devour the bacon, "I don't think Joe's problem is the Mexicans. He's lazy, always working on rusted out cars."

"Well, you have your opinion. I'm going with the brown people."

"Is it that simple? I don't think every Mexican is stealing jobs and killing children. They're a big problem... but, immigration is more complex," Nelson said.

Nelson's father turned off the burner and licked his greasy fingers, "Let me tell you something, son. The Darby's took a boat over to America from England. They wanted hope and a future. Many weeks with little food. But, they came to this country to give, not just take. Not steal and mooch off the government. Everything earned through blood, sweat and tears. That's what this country was founded on. Those Mexicans are takers not givers," he said with a grunt.

Rick Darby worked as a union pipe fitter and made good money in LeClaire. He was close to an early retirement because of an ailing back, from years on the job. His mother was on disability. She had taken a spill at her receptionist job at LeClaire Regional Hospital.

Nelson rolled his eyes and snatched a piece of bacon from the plate. "Dad... You tell this story every week. And the one about walking to school, uphill, both ways, in the snow. But, I think the issues of this country are more complex. There are many minorities who work hard and are trying to make the world a better place. Many people work hard and never become successful. There are a lot of factors beyond our control. Let's not give simple answers to complex situations," Nelson said.

Rick gave a forced smile, "Are you getting soft, son? You know what we stand for in this house. What's going on? I don't like what I'm hearing."

The echoes of Nelson's mother yelling at the TV could be heard in the background. "No. I'm not getting soft. I wonder if we just don't understand the big picture. Many of our beliefs were handed down from our families and never tested, examined, or poked, to explore how true they are. You ever thought about that? Where did your beliefs come from?"

His father paused, rubbed his chin, and dumped a pile of eggs in a bowl, "I have a lot of influences. I grew up in the 50's and 60's, during the Civil Rights Movement. Seen people treated poorly because of the color of their skin. All the worst in people. But, they deserved it. Your grandfather taught me about hard work and not to trust anyone. There are other influences..."

"Then why all the hate toward minorities? I mean, I hate them as much as you. But, where's the room for doubt?"

Nelson's dad bent down and grabbed him by the cheeks. His blue eyes pierced through him, "I have worked hard to put a roof over your head. Literally broke my back to help with college tuition and take care of your mother. Not about to let sweat equity be taken from me because of our liberal government and colored folks. I don't know where these doubts are coming from. But, you need to figure it out if you want a room in this house," Rick said, giving a glare.

Nelson nodded.

Rick reached a high cabinet and pulled down a salt shaker. He poured it on the eggs and a little on the bacon, "I wasn't always this way. Let me say... I've seen stuff. Things I never want my children to experience no matter the cost. You hungry? Let's eat..."

Nelson grabbed a plate from the cupboard and watched his father dump a pile of eggs and bacon on it. He slumped in a chair at the kitchen table.

Rick handed him a flyer, "This afternoon your mother and I are attending a rally. Hosted by American Renaissance. Jarrett Stevens will be speaking. You should come and learn what's happening in this country," he said, with a wink.

Nelson scanned the flyer and his eyes became animated, "Jarrett Stevens? Like this guy. I was reading their magazine last night. Love to go. What time?"

"4 PM. LeClaire Holiday Inn Express in the banquet room. It should be a full house."

Nelson munched on his breakfast and read the flyer a couple more times.

"I knew you were like your father."

Nelson ignored the comment and finished his breakfast.

He walked back into the living room to observe his mother yelling at the screen again, "Buy a vowel, you idiot," she said.

"Wheel of Fortune?" Nelson asked.

"These colored people are morons."

"I'm going back to bed. I don't feel good," Nelson said.

"T... you swamp monkey," his mother said, ignoring Nelson's voice.

6.

J ake Pope hunched toward his computer in the offices of LPD. He was the youngest detective in the history of the department and he found himself in a quandary. Most cases in LeClaire were not high profile and involved murders of spouses and, occasionally, embezzlement. But, this case was big.

A big case considering he had been shipped from LA for grunt work in the small community of Missouri. Not all the details had been revealed, but he was on probation for the work he'd done on a high profile gang case in South Central LA. The crew of LPD didn't welcome Pope as they saw him as a hotshot know-it-all.

He scrolled a news website and examined the face of Jarrett Stevens. A man who leads a racist organization and magazine called American Renaissance. Never charged with any crime. Until now. He's been accused of paying a man in prison to spread the ideologies of AR. A tip inside the prison revealed things are not on the up and up. Pope had been tasked to follow the path of where it might lead and take down Stevens.

Pope tapped on the mouse, let out a sigh, and leaned back in his swivel chair. For all the hours of work on Stevens, strong evidence for an indictment was a pipe dream He wanted to prove himself to the other veteran officers, who were looking over his shoulder and giving him a hard time for being the LA young gun.

"What you looking at?" asked Richard, one of the few black officers on the force.

"Stevens case. He's like a ghost. You'd think with a public personality we'd find something."

Richard nodded and pointed at the website, "Come on Hollywood. You should have this thing solved by now. Give it time and you'll find the link to the chain. Stevens won't get away with his terrorism forever. Justice in this life or the next."

Richard Sterns was a religious man. He had grown up in LeClaire among one of the smallest segments of the population. The African American community. He'd seen racism in small town America when most turned a blind eye. He had attended Kansas University and received his BA in Criminal Justice. He had come back to LeClaire hoping to bring justice to guys like Stevens. He had worked in the department for thirty years.

"Hilarious. You guys think LA is just pretty girls

and famous actors walking down the street. You wouldn't last five minutes."

Sterns backed up from the computer and his large frame hovered over Pope who was much smaller. "Is that so, young buck? You think because you have all the money and fancy technology LA cops are superior?"

"I didn't say that."

"What are you saying Hollywood?"

"What's the population in LeClaire? Like 50,000 if you include surrounding counties. LA has that many people on the same block. More crime per square mile."

"Crime is still crime young blood. You'd be surprised the stuff I've seen in fifteen years. Rape, serial killers, abuse. We live in a broken world, man. You can bet your life on that."

Pope nodded and his eyes didn't leave the computer screen as he scrolled through its content. "All I'm saying is the pace of LeClaire is nothing like LA. We had more going on and more resources to tap into."

"Maybe small town cops are better. Have to rely on skill and instinct. Not resources and technology like you say," Sterns said with a grin.

Pope pushed from the computer and rose to his feet. He glanced up at Sterns, who now had a scowl.

"Don't do anything you'd regret, son."

"I don't want any problems. Just want to do my

job. I'm not looking for competition. I'm looking for help, a partner."

Pope backed down knowing this was not a fight he'd win. But, the rage was still alive. The rage that had gotten him sent to LeClaire.

Sterns held out a strong hand and gave a nod, "Just a little rookie hazing. No problems, bro. I want to take down the racist Jarrett like the rest. More than you."

Pope knew he was right as he had lived a life of privilege. He had a suburban family, lived in Costa Mesa and had attended the best private Catholic Schools. He knew nothing about racism or what it was like to live as a minority in the world.

Jake slapped his hand and smiled. "You're right. A white kid from the burbs is clueless on this stuff. Let's figure it out."

Stevens would be at a rally the next day in LeClaire. That would be a good place to start.

7.

Nelson Darby leaned against the black padded chair in the Holiday Inn Express conference room. The crowd erupted with hoots, hollers, and whistles as Jarrett Stevens took the well lit stage. Queens' "We Will Rock You" blared through speakers.

Jarrett was a handsome man, perfect blonde hair, straight teeth, and tightly ironed Italian suit. No wonder his influence in racist ideologies had spread through American Renaissance. He was easy on the eyes.

"My people, today is a historic day. We are gathered in LeClaire, Missouri, a beacon of hope in a dark world; a place in Civil War history where men fought for their lives to secure the freedoms of this great land. There's nothing that will stop us from pushing our gospel to the forefront of public consciousness; a gospel only the naïve and uniformed will debate. Today, we wake up this sad nation to

33

the dominance of a pure people. A race that has succeeded and thrived in this land for over two hundred years. Today is a day of change..."

The crowd of two hundred exploded in applause and shouts of praise. Rick Darby elbowed Nelson in the ribs. He lowered his camera and raised an eyebrow at his father. "You listening son? Amazing. Listen up; you might learn a thing, or two. Put the stupid camera away," Rick said.

Nelson rolled his eyes and raised the long camera lens of his Canon, taking pictures of Jarrett and the animated crowds. A pit formed in his stomach as he listened to the racist rhetoric bouncing off the walls of the out-dated conference room.

"My team is in search of a new generation of people who'll take this message to the masses. A younger generation that will spread a message of hope to this nation. I'm not getting any younger, and it's time we pass the torch to evangelists who can get things done," Jarrett said, as he waved the microphone.

Nelson jammed the camera in his bag and slouched in the padded chair. Jarrett's eyes locked on his and he felt his stomach churn. He scanned the room, trying to ignore the eye contact.

Nelson turned to his parents; they were glued to the voice and presence of Stevens. They were like kids watching their first movie at a theater.

"This guy's crazy. You buy this stuff?" Nelson asked his father.

Rick whispered. "Your generation must take his message to the world. Stevens' not crazy. He's a genius," he said, turning back to Jarrett who was pumping up the crowds.

Nelson elbowed his father and tried to talk above the now yelling Jarrett. "I don't know if my generation will buy all the rhetoric. Things are changing. To be honest, I'm not sure I buy it, either," Nelson said, bracing himself for a scolding from Rick.

Rick's face was sullen as he looked at Nelson like his hair was on fire. "What'd you say?"

"All the hate. It gets old."

"Old? You do not understand what this man means to our family. His message came in a hard season of life. A time when I questioned everything, like you. No idea the stuff I've seen," he said.

"Dad, please tell me about the stuff. In all the years of ranting about minorities needing to be extinct, you have never told me once what you have supposedly seen. Tell me," Nelson pleaded.

Rick's eyes glazed over and he shook his head. "Not now. We'll talk later. These doubts will pass, they did for me. You'll see the light."

Jarrett winded down his speech and called new recruits to the stage. "If you want to be the generation that takes our message to the masses please come to the stage. I want you to sign this card and someone on our team will follow up. Come... please come, now; no time to wait."

A group of twenty people wandered up to the stage, signed the cards, and were prayed over. Nelson pulled out his camera and documented the prayer ceremony. He thought about the small Pentecostal church he had attended in middle school. The family now rarely attended and had explained it away. Another secret. The people on stage and the vibe of the room felt like church. A little more racism and less Jesus.

"Thank you Lord for creating our perfect race; a pure race called to spread your message to the world. May you continue to purify the earth through us... Amen," Jarrett said, as he opened his eyes.

Nelson watched the tear filled eyes of these recruits. His stomach continued to turn at the words of Jarrett and the conversation with his father. He didn't know what to think anymore.

Detectives Pope and Sterns leaned against a back wall in the corner. Pope took notes and scanned the room. Sterns tried to hold back tears.

8.

Two men in a hurry flashed in front of Nelson's eyes as he nibbled on a cookie at the refreshment table. The room of white people mingled, drinking coffee and replaying Jarrett's speech with hand gestures and animated movements. Nelson observed the crowds with interest.

The two men slammed on the brakes and turned back to Nelson. "Hey, kid. You know where we can find Jarrett Stevens?" asked a man in Wrangler jeans, and a John Deere trucker hat, holding a Confederate flag under one arm.

Nelson smirked and examined the flag. "You'll fit right in with that symbol of racism."

The tall man wearing a John Deere hat smiled and elbowed the wider man. "Not what you think," he said, scratching his unshaven face.

"Isn't that what all racists say? A justification with no answers," Nelson said.

"Excuse me."

"Everyone's in denial these days."

"Including the people who brought me to this crazy rally."

The man wearing the hat folded the flag under his arm and leaned in for a whisper. "Listen. It's not what you think. My partner and I are delivering the flag to Jarrett Stevens. He bought it from our shop. We're antique dealers."

Nelson nodded and showed interest. "Is that symbol of racism worth something?"

"More than your life," the larger man, said with a wink.

"What is this conference? A Klan rally? Jarrett told us to meet him here, no details," the man in the John Deere hat asked.

Nelson smiled and looked around to make sure his father wasn't listening. "Close. Jarrett Stevens is the leader of an organization called American Renaissance. He's recruiting gullible suckers in LeClaire for his racist agenda."

The man scanned the room and adjusted his hat. "Not to be nosy. If this is a room full of racists why are you here? You don't agree with the agenda, do you?"

"Good question. It's complicated. My family dragged me here. Thought I needed enlightenment," Nelson said, with a smile.

"I'm not one to judge. But, must be a rough house to live in. The vibe of this room feels dark."

"I'd be lying if I said the racist leanings in the

home haven't rubbed off on me. But, I'm rethink-ing stuff. College student now. After sophomore year you know everything, right?"

The man in the hat stuck out his hand, stared down at Nelson's camera bag, and pointed at his partner. "Sorry to be rude. Never introduced our-selves. I'm Dexter O'Kane, and this is my business partner, John Wood. You?"

"Nelson Darby," he said, hanging out a dead fish handshake.

Dexter nodded and looked again at the camera bag. "You a photographer?"

"Most days. I'm studying photography at LeClaire Community. You an artist?"

Dexter grinned at John and looked back at Nel-son with something on his mind. "Not an artist, a collector of rusty gold, old stuff. And, Confederate flags," Dexter said, with a half smile.

Nelson forced a smile and didn't seem to under-stand what Dexter meant. "Like a junk collector?"

John butted in, "The junk we sell made us six fig-ures last year. One man's junk, another man's trea-sure."

Nelson lit up, "So you're like those guys on American Pickers on the History Channel, right?"

"Something like that. Let me ask a question. You looking for work? Anytime for a side project when you're not snapping pictures for KKK meetings?" Dexter asked, bumping the camera bag.

"Funny. I'm not working today. Like I said,

dragged here by my parents. What you have in mind?"

"Our shop needs help with our website. It's time to move it from the 90's to the present. Need someone to redesign and shoot pictures of our antiques to sell online. We can't pay a lot, but would love to see what you can do. Interested?"

Nelson's eyes got wide. "Oh, man. That sounds like a fun gig. I love design and shooting photos for the web. Kind of my speciality. But, wait. You made six figures last year. You can't pay much?" Nelson asked.

"I like you. A tough negotiator. We can talk price later. You have a website where we can see your work?" Dexter asked.

Nelson stared at the ground and tapped his blue Converse sneakers. "Ugh, yeah, well, website's down right now. I'll email you pictures of a recent shoot," he said, still staring at the floor.

"You okay, kid?" John asked.

"Yep. I hate showing off work. The artist in me never wants to create just for monetary gain," Nelson said, rummaging through the camera bag and pulling out a business card.

He handed it to Dexter and John and pointed at the contact information. "Ignore the website address for now. Call me and leave an email. I'll send you something."

Dexter yanked an iPhone from the back of his

Wrangler jeans and examined the card. "Done. Texted you my email address."

Nelson smiled and fastened his camera bag closed. "Cool. I'll send you something tonight or first thing tomorrow, okay?"

Dexter and John nodded.

"What's the name of your shop?" Nelson asked.

"Antique Adventures. It's on Main and Green. Come on by and check out the inventory. You seem like a hip college kid. Find something vintage for your dorm room," Dexter said, unfurling the Confederate flag from his arm.

"We need to find this Jarrett character. Time to get paid. This place gives me the creeps," John said, scanning the room.

Nelson's father walked up to the group. "You ready to leave? New friends?"

Nelson stumbled over his words and turned red. "Ugh, not exactly. They're interested in my work."

Rick looked Dexter and John up and down and gave a raised eyebrow. "The picture-taking thing? Seems more like a hobby," he said, rolling his eyes.

Nelson ignored the comment and looked at his sneakers.

"I noticed your flag. You fellas come to hear Jarrett Stevens?" Rick asked.

"Nope. We're here on business and about to leave. The flag is not ours," Dexter said.

"Well, you boys need to consider the teachings from the stage today. You guys look like the type who'd embrace a world changing message. Jarrett Stevens is a modern prophet," he said, rubbing his hands together.

"He sounds a little crazy for my taste. I'm here to pay bills. I'll leave it at that," Dexter said.

"To each his own... Let's go Nelson. Mother's already in the car."

Dexter and John gave a half smile and waved to Nelson as they left the conference room.

"I feel bad. His dad's loony," Dexter said.

"I think the dad might need some enlightening of his own," John said.

9.

The diesel Ford F-150 crawled up the gravel driveway of Antique Adventures. A thirty foot cowboy boot with red tassels greeted Dexter and John on their way into the shop. Dexter reached for the handles of the glass double doors and examined the boot. "You need to sell this thing. I'm tired of looking at it," Dexter said.

"You obviously don't appreciate redneck art," John said, giving Dexter a wink.

"Sell it this month or the boot goes where the sun don't shine."

The antique business was hit or miss. The items, like oversized cowboy boots, may seem like good ideas at the moment, but finding the right buyer was another story. Antique Adventures had been on a good streak and was looking to open another store out of state. But, the boot needed to find a home.

Dexter waved John into the shop like a matador

flagging a bull. He punched the thermostat and dialed up the AC on this abnormally hot spring day. He wiped his head with a red handkerchief hanging from the back pocket of his Wrangler jeans.

"It's hot as shit in here. We need to get the AC looked at. I don't think it's working right," Dexter said.

"I can't tell. I'm always hot with these man breasts," John said, pressing his cleavage together.

"You're hopeless," Dexter said, with a growing smile.

Dexter walked behind a glass counter filled with antique items, from leather gloves to rare jewelry, and fired on the computer. He waited about two minutes and waved John over. "Nelson sent me an email. Come and check out these pictures."

John leaned over Dexter's shoulder, sipping on a thirty-two ounce Cherry Coke. Dexter scrolled through the email attachments and made a moaning sound. "He's good. I don't know what makes a good photographer, but these pictures look solid," Dexter said, pointing to an image of a banana in a bowl.

"That one's making me hungry. You want lunch?" John said, licking his lips.

"Is food all you think about?" Dexter asked.

"No, okay, most of the time. How do you think I keep this girlish figure? I must feed it," John said, rubbing his chest in concentric circles.

Dexter shook his head and ignored the comments. "You want to hire him? I think he would do a good job. Maybe sell the giant boot," Dexter said, rolling his eyes.

"Stop making me feel guilty. I took a chance. Who knew the thirty-foot-boot-market was not there. I'll call Nelson," John said, shaking his thirty two ounce soda, trying to dislodge an ice cube from the side.

John reached into the back pocket of his sweaty Khakis pants. He unfolded a small leather wallet and searched for Nelson's business card. He leaned a cell phone against his swollen cheek. "How much do we pay this kid?" John asked.

"I don't know. What's the going rate for website designers these days?"

John smiled, knowing nothing about the creative side of life. He spent most of his days in a basement doing science experiments on animals. Trying to find the best way to kill things in humane ways. John was more science and less art.

"See what he charges. He probably has a rate sheet," Dexter said, scrolling through more pictures.

John dialed the number and waited a couple beats. "Nelson. John Wood from Antique Adventures. We chatted yesterday about you helping us with a design project. You got a second?"

"Hey, John. Did you get my email?"

"Yes we did. You're good. I think we want to hire

you. What is the going rate for a website guy these days?" John asked, grinning at Dexter, who was sitting on a swivel chair with his hands behind his head.

"Depends on your needs. What does the project entail?"

"Ugh, I don't know. We need a revamped website that looks today, and not 1995. And, pictures of our products to sell online. That shouldn't be that much, right?"

Nelson paused on the line and made a quick estimate in his head. "Let me see. $100 a month for website hosting, which will be on you. Depending on how 1995 the website is, a thousand bucks. And, another $300 for the pictures. Let's call it $1000 even, fair?" Nelson said.

"Holy shit. You're kidding, right? That's how much websites are these days?"

"If you want a good one."

"Does it promise to sell thirty foot cowboy boots?"

"Excuse me."

"Nothing. Let me chat with my partner and call you back. I need to share your pricing. We might need to find a side gig," John said, with a laugh.

"Thanks, Mr. Wood, for the opportunity. You won't be disappointed."

"Better be right. A lot of clams for a website."

John scribbled the price on a slip of paper. He

slid it to Dexter. He asked for thumbs up or thumbs down.

Dexter paused, read the number, and covered his mouth. He mouthed, "Holy shit."

John shrugged.

Dexter gave a reluctant thumb up.

"Hey, Nelson. My partner gave the green light. Come by the shop tomorrow at 9."

"Wonderful," Nelson said.

John hung up the phone and shook his head, still not believing the quoted price. "This website better do my laundry or this guy's fired," John said, staring down Dexter.

"Think of it as charity. We are helping out a broke college student who lives in a crazy racist home."

"I know where I'd like to put that boot now."

"Easy, big fella," Dexter said.

10.

The ceiling fan cut through the mixture of warm Missouri air and the musty bedroom smell of Nelson Darby. He gazed at a Confederate flag hanging on the opposite wall and smiled. He settled further into the comfortable bed and nodded off to sleep.

A small white kid playing basketball dribbled to the right, back to the left, and pretended to score the winning basket on the school playground. The imaginary crowd went wild.

A second white kid with baggy black shorts and long white socks came onto the court and yelled at him.

"Can I play?"

The kid dribbling the basketball paused, looked in his direction, ignored the yell, and fired up a shot that clanked off the orange steel rim. "I don't care. You want to play one on one?"

The other kid pulled up his long white socks,

adjusted his shorts, and smiled. "Cool. I'm Nelson."

"Reggie," the other boy said, exchanging smiles and hand swipes.

"I'm warning you. I'm chain link good," Nelson said.

"We'll see about that," the other kid said, firing up a shot that swished in the center of the net.

The kid's laughed and showed one another their best moves on a warm summer day in Missouri. The sunset and the cicadas sang in unison.

Both boys sat on their basketballs and wiped sweat from their red faces. "What school you go to?"

"Boone Elementary, you?"

"Home schooled."

"What's that like?"

"You spend a lot of time with your mom. That is not always that cool," Reggie said, with a smile.

Nelson smiled and gazed at the pink sky, blazing with color in the East. "I better get home. It's almost time for dinner."

"Yeah, me too."

The boys walked toward the chain link fence with a gate that led out onto the sidewalk. A couple of kids with sagging jeans came into view and blocked the entrance.

"Where you honkeys going?"

Nelson looked at Reggie and his smile turned to a frown. "We don't want no trouble. We're just heading home," Nelson said, as he tried to walk around the kid blocking the entrance.

One of the kid's looked down at the basketball in Nelson's arm and smiled. "You think you can play basketball? You're just a bunch of dorky white kids."

Nelson didn't know whether to laugh or defend himself. He looked at Reggie for some kind of response. "I'm okay, but, Reggie here is the bomb. He whipped my butt playing one on one."

"Is that right?" a black kid said, hiding behind the kid blocking the entrance. He was sipping on a can of soda.

"Yep. I don't know if I even scored five points on him."

The boys scanned Reggie up and down and smiled at his blue basketball shorts with holes and sagging white athletic socks. "He looks poor. Homeless," the boy said elbowing his partner.

"Knock it off. We want no trouble," Reggie said, sticking out his chest in confidence.

"No trouble. But, I have been looking for something."

"What's that?" Nelson asked.

"I need a new basketball. Mine is getting old. Looks like you have one. Give me the ball and we'll be on our way."

Reggie glanced at Nelson, his lip trembled with fear, and gripped the ball tighter under his arm. "This is my ball. The only one I got."

"Cause you poor?" the second boy said laughing.

"No. This is my brother's."

"Good. He won't mind if I take it."

The larger kid threw an overhand right into the cheek of Reggie. His head whipped to the side, and the ball bounced on the black pavement. Nelson reached for the ball and felt a stab in his stomach.

The smaller kid had punched Nelson in the gut. All the air knocked out of Nelson as he tried to look up and speak with little words. "That's his ball. Give it back," Reggie said.

The two kids stood back in pride and the one dribbled the ball between his legs and spun it on his finger. "This is how it's done. Thanks for the ball."

Nelson regained his composure and watched the boys passing the ball back and forth, smiling like they had won a war. He glided over to the boys and stood in front of them.

"I want the ball back. It doesn't belong to you."

"Go to hell, white boy."

"I will not ask again. Give me the ball back or this will end badly."

The adrenaline from the punch to the gut and the rush of excitement pumped through Nelson's veins. His face was red and sweaty.

The smaller boy looked at the other and smirked. "I don't want to have to punch you in the gut again. This time I will go for the face" he said, looking at Reggie on the ground.

Reggie lay on the ground and moaned as blood dripped from the corner of his lip.

"I will take that basketball back. I don't want to use force."

"Weird thing to say after you both just got the crap beaten out of you."

"I will not repeat myself," Nelson said.

The two black kids approached Nelson and stood a foot from his face. He could feel their breath on his face. "This is our ball white boy. We don't like your kind. Never talk this way."

"I don't like your kind. Swamp trash."

"What?"

"You heard me. Swamp trash is what my father calls black people. You are just dirty swamp dwellers like catfish. No good and useless."

"You can tell your dad to kiss my black ass."

The boys jumped on Nelson and punched him in the face and back and kicked his face in. They didn't stop until Nelson blacked out.

Nelson shot up from a cold sweat and scanned the dark bedroom. The ceiling fan blew on his sweaty forehead.

Damn. The dream, again.

11.

Nelson parked at the entrance of Antique Adventures and yanked the rearview mirror to examine the black bags under his eyes. He sipped a twenty ounce coffee and sighed. The camera bag was sitting in the passenger seat, strapped in with a seatbelt like a baby.

He undid the belt, slung the bag over his slender frame, and yanked on his sagging jeans. Nelson opened the glass doors and was hit with a rush of cold air. Dexter and John stared down at different newspapers and popped up their heads like members of a trained synchronized swimming team when he appeared.

Dexter saluted, "Hey, Darby. Long time no see," he said, looking at a black wristwatch and then tapping the screen, "Right on time. I like that in an employee. Something others could learn," glaring at John, glued to the newspaper.

Nelson readjusted his camera case and looked

up with drooping eyes, "Morning. Thanks again for the opportunity. I need to build my portfolio for college and this will help a ton," he said, slinging his black case on the glass counter.

Dexter waved him behind the counter and cleared out a space to work, "Take a look at the current website," Dexter said, turning the monitor toward Nelson.

"Oh, my word. You weren't kidding. This site is straight from the 90's. Like the neon colors. Elevator music a nice touch," Nelson said, rolling his eyes and trying to hold back a laugh.

"Is there hope?" Dexter asked.

"The beauty of the internet age. You can reboot anytime you like. I'll use my magic and design a website from this decade in no time."

John walked over and glanced at the screen. "Yeah, that thing is awful. Who does our website anyway, Dexter?"

Dexter raised a slow hand and smiled. He reached under the counter and yanked out a five hundred page book. "Websites for Dummies. The guy at the store said anyone could build a site. I tried to save the shop a few bucks," he said, tossing the book under the counter.

"Now we can pay this child $1000 to design a website from this era. Smart business move," John said, hitting Dexter in the arm.

Nelson stepped back from the wretched website and scanned the inside of the shop. He pointed to the left and the right. "All these items adorning the shelves and tables. You want them online?"

Dexter's eyes became animated and walked out in front of the counter. He stopped in front of a table covered in vintage leather clothing. He held up a jacket. "You see this bad boy?"

"Yeah, the 80's called and want their leather jacket back," Nelson said, looking at John for affirmation. He didn't smile.

"Funny, kid. This is a Harley Davidson jacket from the 60's. How much is it worth?" Dexter asked.

Nelson came from behind the counter, grabbed the jacket, and placed it up against his stomach. "About my size. Fifty bucks give or take."

"How 'bout the cost of a redesigned website," Dexter said, with a wide mouthed smile.

Nelson placed the jacket back on the table and covered his mouth. "You're shitting me. A grand?"

"What people think out of date is rusty gold, for us. People from around the world call and email us about this stuff. Why we need your help. Get the word out. Make us money," Dexter said, rubbing his fingers together.

Nelson raised his eyes and turned around, inspecting the items perched around the shop. "Who knew this junk would be worth so much. Forget photography, I need to be in the junk selling business."

John stood with his hands akimbo and shook his

index finger side to side. "Never call us junk collectors. We are antique dealers."

"My bad."

Nelson slid back to the camera case, pulled out a medium sized lens, and raised the camera to the ceiling. He moved around the shop snapping pictures of leather jackets, gas signs, and train lights. He took another shot, glanced down at his LCD screen, and took another one smiling as he went. John and Dexter sat back and admired the ability of the young man.

"I can tell you have passion for photography. You smile when you work," Dexter said.

Nelson turned the camera LCD screen toward Dexter. "Presto. I think they might work for the website. I'll touch them up."

Dexter nodded and passed the camera to John. He smiled and handed it back to Nelson. "I think you'll be a great asset to the team."

Dexter slapped John in the head. "Who says asset? This is an informal company. Nelson will be a great addition to the team."

John stuck out his tongue, "Sorry for trying to class up this place."

Dexter didn't respond.

Dexter gave John a wink. Their smiles turned to seriousness. "There's one thing we need to chat about. John and I have one concern."

Nelson gently placed the camera back in the bag

and looked up, "What's that? Is it my prices? I can make you a deal. I really want this job."

"No, price is fine," Dexter hesitated, and tried to form the words, "The rally the other day. We don't want our shop associated with any kind of racist agenda. We want our company to operate with integrity. The message of Jarrett Stevens does not match our values. You understand, right?"

Nelson jammed his hands into his jean pockets, "I'm embarrassed to be associated with those people. Don't think less of me."

"I don't want to judge your motivations. We all do stupid things. You were at the Jarrett Stevens rally. That means something, doesn't it?"

"It does. I live in a home where these ideals are passed down like gospel truth. Trying to separate myself from it. Don't worry. I won't bring any weirdness to work. Work is work."

"We are nervous hiring someone who might spread that message to the people in our community. Not what we stand for as a company. You understand our hesitation?"

"Yes, sir. Wouldn't want to cause any harm to you, or your business. Promise to focus on the work and nothing else. I have no agenda. I want to design websites, take excellent pictures, and build my portfolio. Trust me."

Dexter glanced at John, who stood with arms crossed listening to the conversation. "I have a good vibe about you. But, any weird stuff and you're gone. No questions asked. Got it?"

Nelson nodded and reached out a hand. "I'll make a list of what we need to do first. I'll send an invoice and get started right away," he said, shaking Dexter's hand, and then John's.

Nelson turned to leave the shop and shot back with a question. "Did you ever find Jarrett Stevens? He like the flag?" Nelson asked.

Dexter nodded. "He was a piece of work. Wants to buy more stuff from the shop. I can deal with his racist nonsense if it makes me money."

Nelson grinned. "Be careful with that guy. Looks can be deceiving."

Dexter saluted, "Thanks, kid. See you tomorrow."

12.

Nelson reached for his buzzing cell phone on the end table in his bedroom, "What do you want? We doing anything tonight?" Nelson asked, adjusting his jeans next to his bed.

"A new club opened downtown. There's supposed to be a rap group playing tonight. Let's go."

Nelson smiled and then sighed, "You know how I feel about rap."

"You racist bastard. Not everyone believes what you believe, friend. A little rap music will not hurt you. Broaden your racist horizons. Art is art."

"A bunch of thugs talking about bitches, hoes, and shooting police officers. Not my idea of art," Nelson said, picking up an AC/DC album.

"Better than the white supremacist and devil worship music you listen to."

"Heavy metal is not devil music. They are artists expressing the deeper angst and desires of youth culture. At least they play their own instruments."

"Shut up. You want to come, or not?"

Nelson paused, shook his head, and shot back. "Fine. If the music sucks, we're leaving. I'm bringing Led Zeppelin for the car ride."

"I'll pick you up in twenty."

Nelson hung up the phone and packed his camera bag with a couple extra lenses. He never left the house without the camera for fear of missing artistic moments, as he called them.

Nelson sat on the curb as the white Nissan Pathfinder pulled to a screeching halt. A red-haired kid yelled from the driver side. "Hop in loser. You bring your devil music?"

Nelson settled into the passenger seat and pulled a CD from the side compartment of his camera case. "This, my friend, is rock-and-roll. Pure and simple. The best music ever produced in the history of the world."

Chad Morton was Nelson's best friend since life's first breath. Their families used to be friends until the Darby's became more involved in American Renaissance and stopped going to church. Chad was loyal despite the change in Nelson.

Nelson gave devil horns as Cashmere played through the speakers. "This is real music. Engages the soul," he said, bobbing his head up and down.

"At least have an open mind tonight. You might not like the music but, at least, do it for your best buddy."

"The only reason I'm here. I need the company."

"What's up?" Chad asked, turning down the radio.

"My folks took me to a Renaissance rally the other day."

"Oh. The racist rally?"

"A misconception. Mostly about politics and race in our country. Jarrett Stevens is a smart dude."

"If Jarrett Stevens is smart. I'm Einstein."

"Whatever. I'm in a weird place. Belief system hazy. Agreed with a lot of what Stevens said. A lot is hard to swallow."

"You need to get back to church. That would help with the searching. Hear another perspective."

"Organized religion is what I need like a hole in my head."

Chad shook his head and pulled a cigarette from his shirt pocket. "Church is not for perfect people. At least our message is love not hate. I'll take my organized religion over the nonsense of Jarrett Stevens any day," he said, pushing in the car lighter, and offering one to Nelson.

Nelson held the cigarette in his fingers and stared out the window. "My problem. I know the message of Stevens is confusing. It's all I've known. His message is the message of my family. It kind of gets its hooks in you and doesn't let go."

"We all can change our minds about stuff. Like

rap music being a superior art form than heavy metal," Chad said, blowing smoke in Nelson's face.

"Knock it off, asshole. I'll put up with it for a night. No more, or friendship is over," Nelson said, lighting his cigarette.

13.

Nelson and Chad pulled up in front of Club Nemo as a crowd of young people waited in line.

"Doesn't look like many heavy metal fans here tonight," Chad said, with a wink.

Nelson watched a group of African American kid's stare him down as they drove by. "Is this a wise idea?"

"Keep your mouth shut and enjoy the music. We'll be fine."

Nelson and Chad made it into the club and stood at the back, watching the stage. A group called Thug Life danced and invited the crowd to sing along.

Chad elbowed Nelson. "I love these guys. Let's move to the front."

Nelson shook his head in reservation. "No way. I'm fine right here," he said, leaning against a back wall near the bathrooms.

"Come on, man. It smells back here. The right side of the stage has room. You need to feel the music, not just hear it."

"I can hear plenty from here."

"All right. Suit yourself. I'm going to the front," Chad said, pushing aside people and finding a spot at the right side of the stage.

Nelson scanned the room of predominately black and Latino young people, surprised by the diversity in the small town of LeClaire. He looked at his watch and fiddled with his camera bag strap.

He sighed and reached into the bag to attach a lens to the camera. These people are fascinating creatures.

Nelson glanced to the left and examined a young girl grinding, with her boyfriend, to the music. He veered to the right and watched two young guys jumping to the beats of the music. He smiled and snapped pictures, not paying attention to the music or the strange looks people were giving him.

Chad waved from the front of the stage, gesturing for Nelson to come forward.

Nelson ignored the request and kept taking pictures of the dancing audience.

A tall black man rubbed up against Nelson. "What's the deal with the camera? You never been to a club before, white boy?"

Nelson dropped the camera to his side and smiled. "I find this whole thing fascinating."

"What do you mean fascinating? You never seen black people at a concert before?"

"Rarely."

"What you gonna do with the pictures? You some kind of pervert?"

"Excuse me."

"You heard me. I don't like you taking pictures of my girl."

"I don't know what you're talking about?" Nelson pleaded.

The man leaned into Nelson and pointed down at the camera slung over his shoulder. "You heard me white boy. I saw you taking a picture of me and my girl when we was dancing. You going to put this on the internet or Facebook?"

Nelson leaned back and tried to create space between himself and the man breathing in his face. He raised his hands. "I don't want trouble. I'm a photographer taking pictures. Nothing weird."

"Give me your camera. I want to delete all your pictures."

"I don't think so."

"Give me the camera or this gets serious."

Nelson's forehead beaded up with sweat and he shuffled his feet, gripping the camera. "I will leave now. I don't need this..." Nelson said and tried to step away.

The man grabbed his camera and ripped it off his shoulder as the bag fell to the ground. He held up the camera in Nelson's face. "Erase the pictures or I break this thing in half," he said, raising the camera in the air.

Nelson reached up for the camera. "I can't erase these pictures. I need them."

"You got five seconds to choose. Erase the pictures or you'll be buying a new camera."

Nelson paused and gave a half smile. "I can't. You people are fascinating creatures. I need it for my project."

Chad walked over and stood in front of Nelson. "What's going on? Why didn't you join me up front?"

"Who's this? Back up," the man said to Chad.

He turned to the man. "We don't want any trouble, dude."

"Your little friend here is taking pictures of me and my girl. He needs to erase the pictures or I will bust him up."

Chad looked down at the camera. "Shit, Nelson. You brought that thing in here. Erase the pictures. Let's not make a scene."

"No. Screw this guy. This is a free country. If I want to take a picture of fascinating people, let me be."

"Fascinating people? What are you saying?"

"What I thought," the black man said.

"I'm taking pictures for my latest project."

"Erase the pictures," Chad said, trying to hold off the man.

The man gripped Nelson by the neck and pulled

him toward the front door of the club. "I'm tired of this shit. You coming with me."

Chad trailed behind, yelling for him to stop.

"Don't do anything you'll regret," Nelson said, his camera bag swinging off his back.

"All you had to do was erase the pictures."

The man dragged Nelson to the alley at the side of the club. He gripped the camera strap and swung it up against a brick wall. The plastic of the camera shattered and sprayed the ground. He then tossed the camera bag in a dumpster.

"I told you to erase the pictures. Now I did it for you," the man said flashing a gold tooth.

Nelson knelt down over the shattered camera and looked up at the man with a tear coming from his eye. "You asshole. Why would you do this? I wasn't trying to hurt anyone."

He snickered. "Who's fascinating now, chump."

Nelson lunged at the man and swung with a wild right hand missing his face. He shifted to the right and grabbed Nelson around the neck. Punched him in the cheek and tossed him to the ground. Eight more kicks to the gut for good measure.

Nelson rolled around on the ground and tried to protect himself from further punches.

The man disappeared back into the club.

Chad stood over Nelson and gathered the remnants of the camera on the alley floor.

"Dammit, Nelson. Why didn't you just erase the pictures?"

"They're fascinating people. I needed them for my project," Nelson said, spitting out blood onto the cement.

Chad ignored the comment and picked him up from the ground.

"You need serious help."

14.

Nelson rocked in the worn recliner, pressing a bag of frozen peas against his swollen face. The light of a passerby shone through the front room of the dark house. He pushed on the ground to make the chair stop rocking, raising pain in his stomach muscles.

"How was tonight?" Nelson's mother asked, pulling her pink nightgown across her chest.

Nelson rocked and tried to ignore the questions, staring down at the label on the bag of peas. "Fine. Chad took me to a club downtown to listen to a band."

"Heavy metal?"

Nelson smiled and placed the peas on his other cheek. "I wish. Would've been safer. Black people music, rap."

His mother glided in closer and clicked on a lamp on an end table. She covered her mouth with her hands. "What the hell happened to your face?"

Ryan J. Pelton

"You should see the other guy."

"Who did this to you? Chad?"

"No."

"Then who?"

"Some dude at the club."

"A black dude?"

"Yeah."

Nelson's mother slammed her small wrist on the table as a family picture tipped over. "Dammit, Nelson. Why did he hurt you? Tell me now."

"I took his picture."

"Why in the hell did you take a picture of a swamp monkey?"

"Bored with the music and wanted to capture the moment. What photographers do."

"The moment. Those swamp monkeys don't deserve your attention," she said, rubbing a large cut on his right cheek.

"They're fascinating."

"What?"

"I find that species interesting to take pictures of."

She put the back of her hand on his forehead. "You sick son? Nothing about those people is worth taking pictures of. They need erasing from the planet."

"My take is different. You and dad raised me to think a certain way. These people are interesting. I am not sure what this means or what it says about me. They are intriguing humans."

72

"Those people just beat the shit out of you. You don't think that means something? What does it say about the species? They are violent animals."

"I deserved it."

"What did you do?"

Nelson placed the bag of peas on the table and leaned back in the recliner. "He wanted me to erase the pictures I took. I didn't want to."

"The monkey beat you up because you took his picture and wouldn't erase it? Why didn't you do it?"

Nelson shrugged, "I wanted to keep the pictures. Like I said, they are fascinating people."

"Well, regardless, he had no right to hurt you in this way. I'm going to tell your father and let him take care of it."

Nelson looked up hard and his lip bent down. "Please don't tell dad. I want to let this go."

"I don't need any more drama around the situation. You know how he feels about swamp people."

"I will make something up, please, mom."

Nelson's mother picked up the peas and leaned over the recliner to place them on his left cheek. "Nelson, you're questioning things. Tonight should be confirmation of everything we prize and believe in as a family. This is only more kindling for the fire."

"What fire, mom? What in the hell is the end game? You think you are going to kill everyone who doesn't have white skin? Is that the plan?"

"Please don't raise your voice at me son. I want you to consider your beliefs and how they affect this home. Your father and I have been talking about you."

"What did he say?"

"He told me you have been questioning your faith?"

"Faith? We hardly attend church."

"The teachings of Jarrett Stevens are our Holy Book. We adhere to the world domination of American Renaissance. He is our prophet," she said, with a crooked smile and raised eyebrow.

Nelson placed his head against the recliner and put his hands behind his head. "I went to the rally. I read the magazines."

"Then why is any of this hard to understand?"

Nelson bit his thumb nail. "I don't want to end up like Danny."

Mrs. Darby backed away, set the peas on a coffee table, and raised an eyebrow. "Danny? Why would you ever speak ill of your own brother? He at least adheres to the faith of the family."

"How'd that work out?"

She slapped Nelson across the face.

Nelson gave out a scream and turned to the side. "What the hell, mom? You've always favored Danny."

"Don't speak about your brother in that way. You have it easy young man."

Nelson grabbed the peas and stared at the floor,

the throbbing in his face intensifying. "Sorry. I'm sure jail has taught Danny many life lessons."

"Good night, Nelson. Sleep it off. We can talk about this later."

Nelson reached into a magazine rack next to the recliner. He picked up a copy of American Renaissance and scanned a couple pages. He tossed it on the floor and went to bed.

He listened to a Led Zeppelin album before fading to sleep.

15.

Danny Darby slid the cash across the counter and grabbed the unfiltered American Spirit cigarettes from the pimply faced cashier. His swastika tattoo on his right forearm caught the cashier's eye.

"Oh shit. You, Danny Darby?" he asked, holding out a fist for a bump.

Danny nodded and gave a weak half smile. "Yep. Do I know you?"

"Rickey Rogers. I went to Greeley High with your brother, Nelson."

He nodded.

"Where you been? I heard you were in the joint?"

"True."

"When did you get out?"

"An hour ago."

"Damn. What was that like?"

"I don't recommend it."

The cashier nodded and scanned Danny up and down. "Welcome back to LeClaire. You want to hang out sometime?"

Danny nodded, with no intentions of ever hanging with anyone who went to school with his younger brother. Danny was not the socializing type and worked best in isolation. He was a loner.

The full size Dodge Ram truck sat idle at the curb as Danny jumped in the passenger side. He looked over at his dad and smiled. "Thanks for stopping. It's been a while since I sucked on one of these," Danny said, lighting up the American Spirit.

Danny's father smiled and slapped him on the knee and shook his head a couple times. "Son, I never thought we'd see you again. This is a happy day..."

Danny nodded.

"You look strong, kid. Any trouble with swamp monkeys in the joint?"

"Nothing I couldn't handle."

"You need to smack your brother around. He's questioning stuff."

"What do you mean?"

"The family faith is being questioned. Nelson thinks he's above all we hold dear. That book learning in college is messing up his mind. I took him to a Jarrett Stevens rally to help him think through stuff."

"How'd that go?"

"Still the same. Head and heart hard."

"I'll talk to him," Danny said, blowing smoke out the truck window and rubbing the swastika on his arm.

"How's mom?"

"Pain in my ass. She's at home because of a hurt ankle. I need her back at work. The nagging is getting old."

"Nice part of prison. No nagging women," Danny said, with a slow smile.

Danny's father nodded, imagining life without his wife.

"What's Nelson up to, besides questioning our faith?" Danny asked.

"Taking pictures. Which got his ass beat up last night at a club downtown."

"Really?"

"Chad took him to a new club to listen to some black people music. He was taking pictures of people at the club. Someone beat the shit out of him in the alley."

"Black guy?"

"Yep."

Danny took a deep drag on the cigarette and stared deep into his father's eyes. " Unacceptable. I think we might need to find this guy and pay him a visit."

"Don't be stupid. You just got out of the joint. Let Nelson deal with his own bullies. You need to cool off. The last time we took matters into our own hands you got busted."

"I'm smarter now."

"How so?"

"When you're young, you react with physical force. I am learning to use my mind more than my brawn."

His dad reached over and gripped Danny's ripped bicep and squeezed. "Damn. You must've spent a lot of time lifting weights in prison," Rick said, with a grin.

"Nothing else to do. That and steer clear of gang fights."

"Your brother will be excited to see you."

Danny nodded. "We need to talk. I don't like what I'm hearing about him. Sounds like he's getting soft. I'll talk sense into him."

Danny's father turned on his signal and pulled out onto Main Street in downtown LeClaire. He gave one more punch to Danny's solid arm. "Welcome home, son. I missed you."

Danny nodded and took a drag of the cigarette.

16.

N elson grabbed the front door of his ranch style house as the door pushed back on him. He locked eyes with a tall, strong man, smiling from ear to ear.

"Brother! How the hell are you?"

Nelson backed up and examined Danny, up and down, having forgotten what he looked like. Five years was a long time. Definitely wasn't as buff.

"Wow. Big brother has come home. I never thought I'd see the day. Shit, you're huge. You doing steroids?"

"All natural, little bro. Got to stay strong to fight off bad guys."

Nelson gave a smile and leaned in for a hug. "Glad you're home. How was the joint?"

"Lonely. I missed punching my brother in the head," Danny said, slapping him across the back of the head.

"What the hell?"

"I heard you're giving mom and dad crap. Questioning the faith?"

Nelson backed away and shook his head, looking at his dad to the left of Danny. "They told you?" he asked, giving his father a stare.

"Yeah, dad told me. I don't like hearing this shit. Why did I spend the last five years of my life in jail? For everything we believe in as a family."

"Whatever helps you sleep at night. Not everything is black and white."

Danny pressed in and grabbed Nelson's shoulder with a firm grip. He winced in pain. "What did you say, you little shit? Those people deserved what they had coming. I hope you understand the sacrifice I made for this cause. You need to wake up, kid."

Nelson ripped his arm away. "Give me room for doubt, okay. Anyway... Glad you're home and hope you find whatever you're looking for."

Danny swiped the side of Nelson's face where there were cuts and a bruise. "Who did this to you?"

"Nobody."

"Dad told me otherwise. Black people hurt you?"

"What does it matter the color of their skin?"

"It matters. It always matters."

"A black dude hit me. I deserved it."

"Why did he hurt you?"

"I took his picture."

"Dad told me you're into photography. What's that about?"

"I'm studying photography in school. I like it."

Danny nodded and placed his hand on top of Nelson's short hair. "You getting soft? Artists are usually gay. You gay?"

"Shut up. Not all artists are gay. I'm not getting soft. Just into different things now," Nelson said, trying to not stare Danny in the face.

"You used to be into girls, basketball, and boxing. What happened?"

"Dudes can't like art? Prison obviously didn't beat the asshole out of you."

"Why were you taking pictures of this black guy? What a waste of film."

"I was bored."

"Where did this happen?"

"Club Nemo with Chad. He wanted to see a band."

"Black music."

Nelson nodded.

"Why did this monkey take a shot at you?"

"I didn't want to erase my pictures of him and his girlfriend."

"Why not?"

"I don't like erasing pictures. I use them for stuff."

"For what?"

"My website. I think minorities are fascinating people."

Danny shook his head and tried to bite his lip and not boil over with rage. "What the hell? There's nothing fascinating about black people. They are what is wrong with this city, state, nation, and world. You know that..."

"Whatever."

"So, you think a dude beats the shit out of you for taking his picture, and that is okay. That is what's wrong with these people. They are angry and think it's okay to feel superior to the greater race."

"Oh, the irony. Who's angry? Who went to jail because he couldn't keep his anger in check?" Nelson asked.

Danny pressed Nelson against the living room wall and jammed his forearm into his neck. "You be careful kid. I got sent to jail for the honor of this family. Damned if I will let my little ass, unenlightened brother talk shit when those people pound in his face. You're delusional. Anger justified."

Rick stood in front of the brothers and gave a nervous smile. "Hey kids. Let's not worry about this. Danny is home and we need to celebrate. We are going out to eat tonight, Chelly's."

Danny put his hands up in surrender, backed away from Nelson and smiled. He then came back in for a hug from his brother. "We're cool. I need time to adjust to life outside the joint. You understand, right?" Danny said, winking at Nelson.

Nelson and his father nodded. "We are all a little

shocked that you got out of prison and you need time to adjust to this new life," Rick said.

Danny wrapped his arm around Nelson and pulled him in close. "I need to reconnect with my little brother. I can't believe he's in college. The last time I saw him he was spanking his monkey and popping pimples. They grow up fast."

"I'll get mother and pull the car up. Who wants Mexican?"

Danny shook his head and smiled. "I care little for the people. Sure can cook though."

17.

The Darby family chattered around the red vinyl booth at Chelly's. It was the only worthy Mexican restaurant in LeClaire, according to Nelson. Mariachi music played loudly in the background.

Danny dipped a tortilla chip in a bowl of salsa and smiled across the table. "How are your grades, kid?" Danny asked, looking at Nelson.

"Fine."

"Like fine passing with a C, or fine thriving with A's and B's."

"B's"

"I don't know how he gets B's taking photography classes," Rick said, with a smirk.

"Easy dad. The Darby's aren't the intellectual types. You barely graduated high school," Danny said.

"I went to the school of hard knocks. I made a living with little education. College is just a brainwashing machine. Those professors are selling lies," Rick said.

The table ignored his rant.

"I don't think grade point averages are the proof someone is smart. Professors are doing their best. I wouldn't make such blanket statements," Nelson said, dipping a chip in the salsa.

"You gotta have street smarts or you will get your ass killed. You can't measure that on no multiple choice test," Danny said, wiping his mouth of salsa, and sipping a beer.

"Danny... Any girls for Nelson to date? He needs to find a girlfriend," their mother said.

Nelson blushed and swirled a chip in the bowl, staring down at the table. "Mom... I'm busy with school. Give me a break."

Danny said, "A couple girls from high school he'd like. They're a little older. An experienced woman makes a man quick," he said, elbowing his father to the right of the table.

"Let's talk about something else," Nelson said.

"Okay. How about why you're getting soft? Why you got your face pounded in by a swamp monkey." Danny said.

"How 'bout not."

"You embarrassed?"

"No. I want to let it go, that's all."

Danny leaned over the table and softened his tone. "The Darby family ain't a bunch of pussies. Damned if you will make this family look bad."

Nelson looked at his mother and then father. "What does that even mean? Am I supposed to fight every minority in this town when they look at me funny?" Nelson asked.

"Only if they deserve it," Danny said, looking at his dad for affirmation.

Rick nodded.

Nelson glanced across the restaurant and saw a man eating with a girl. He quickly stared down and propped open a menu to cover his face.

Danny looked back over his shoulder.

"What did you see? You look spooked."

"Nothing."

Danny scanned the restaurant and examined the ten tables around the room. "An old girlfriend? Your face is red."

"Don't worry about it."

Nelson pulled the menu down and read it for what he wanted to eat. He peeked over the edge to a far table.

"You keep looking at that dude in the back. Is he the one who hurt you?" Danny asked.

Nelson locked eyes on the man and he stood from the table.

He sauntered over. The black man stood calmly with his hands behind his back.

"Huh... Small world, wouldn't you say?"

Nelson hunched his shoulders and tried to be small in the booth. "I guess so. I think bigger that we think. LeClaire can make it feel that way."

"Funny guy. Amnesia? The club last night?"

"No. Probably confused with a different white dude."

"Few white dudes. I'm sure I'd remember. How did you get those cuts?"

"Fell off my bike."

"No... No... I am sure you're the asshole who kept taking my picture. When I asked you to stop and erase the pictures well... you got your face pounded," he said, pointing to Nelson's face.

Danny rose from the table, placed his napkin down, and widened his arms. "Is there a problem here? My family is trying to eat our dinner."

The man stepped back and raised his hands in surrender. "No problem. I wanted to say hi to an old friend."

"Friend? We ain't friends with your kind."

"My kind?"

"Yes, your kind. The inferior kind."

The man inched closer to Danny and didn't back down. "I'd be careful, partner. Not sure what kind of racist group you're part of. But, I will do what I did to your brother," he said, examining the swastika on Danny's forearm.

"Please, Danny. Sit down. Our food will come soon. Not tonight," the mother said.

"I'm almost done, ma. We're just chatting."

Danny leaned into the ear of the black man and whispered. He recoiled, "Why don't we chat out-side?"

The two men glided out of the restaurant and Nelson sank into the booth. "You going to say something Rick?" mother asked.

"Nope. Let them handle this like men."

"You need to do something."

Rick tossed his napkin on the table, got up from his seat, and followed them to a side alley next to the restaurant. He unhinged the trunk of the car and yanked out a bat.

Danny and the black man stood toe to toe in the alley. "You ready to have your face bashed in like your brother?" the man asked.

"Not today. My brother's soft. I ain't nothing like him."

Danny raised his right arm and was about to come down with a right hook and the man fell to the ground in a heap. His dad stood over him, spinning the baseball bat between his fingers. "Home Run."

Danny stood wide eyed and smiled, looking at the black man whose head was bleeding from the back. "I didn't think you still had it in you."

"It never goes away."

Danny gave his father a high five. He wiped the blood from the end of the bat, placed it in the trunk of the car, and walked back into the restaurant.

They both giggled as they entered the restaurant and acted as if nothing had happened.

"What happened?"

"We took care of it," Danny said.

"What do you mean?" mother asked.

"The swamp monkey won't be bothering us any longer," Danny said, scanning his menu.

"Who wants burritos? Best in LeClaire," Danny said, glancing at Nelson, slumped in the booth and covering his face.

18.

Nelson raised the camera to focus in on an old bicycle hanging from the wall. He snapped a couple pictures and glided around the shop in Antique Adventures. He stared down at the LCD screen to check the last picture and nodded, with a smile.

John leaned over the glass counter and flipped through the LeClaire Gazette. He raised an eyebrow and held up the front page story to Dexter.

"Look who's out of jail," John said, pushing the paper in Dexter's face.

"Thank you. I can read just fine. My eyes are not bad like yours."

John stuck out his tongue and adjusted the glasses hanging off the end of his nose. "I hate these things. I made it thirty-five years without corrective lenses. Damn eye doctors taking my money. Those guys are scam artists. I'll switch to contacts soon, for the ladies..."

Dexter shook his head and scanned the newspaper. "I remember this guy. He got thrown in jail for assaulting a black kid in town. I think he was part of a white supremacist group. Forget the name," Dexter said, skimming the article.

John nodded. "Oh yeah, the article said there was some shady lawyering going on. He should've got more time because the kid died. Beat him so badly he was paralyzed from the neck down and then died a few months later. Sad. Should've gotten more time than five years. Not sure how that happens?"

Nelson danced around the room and pretended not to listen to the conversation between the guys. Dexter mouthed the words in the article. "Nelson. Your last name 's Darby. You related to this guy?" Dexter asked, flipping the paper around and aiming it toward Nelson.

Nelson shook his head and went back to shooting. He raised the camera up and took a picture of a Shell Gas sign in the middle wall of the shop. He placed the camera on the counter and waved John over. "This what you want?"

"Whoa... Those photos are amazing. This rusty gold looks a million times better on the camera. Get this stuff online soon and we will be rich," John said, smiling and playing with his glasses.

Nelson smiled.

Dexter came over to the camera and peeked at the Shell sign. "Wonderful. You sure this guy isn't related to you? I don't want bad press coming around the shop if he's your kin. We don't need more help to lose money. I think what he did to that kid is beyond sick. He should've rotted in jail for the rest of his life. The political system can be a pile of shit," Dexter said, shaking his head, and closing the paper.

John shot back, "I agree. Last week I got a ticket for parking in front of fire hydrant. I went into Rudy's to get the usual. The officer wrote me a ticket after only being inside for five minutes. You kidding me?"

"You sure it was only five minutes, fatty," Dexter said, rubbing John's bloated stomach.

"I love their milkshakes. Best in LeClaire," John said, licking his lips.

"When justice works, it's a beautiful thing. When it fails, like with this kid, it makes me sick to my stomach," Dexter said.

"You ever think of running for office," Nelson asked.

Dexter said, "I'd be angry most of the day. Dealing with the red tape and political BS. People say they would love to be President and make America great. The worst job on the planet. Nobody can really change anything. Why I like taking things into my own hands," Dexter said, reaching for a hand slap from John.

"Probably better pay than this dump," John said, holding back from the hand slap.

"Speaking of pay. You get my invoice? I'm almost done with the website rebuild. All the pictures will be online later today," Nelson said.

Dexter pressed a button on the cash register, and the drawer slipped open. He thumbed through a wad of bills and threw them on the counter. "This work?"

Nelson stared at the wad and smiled, thumbing it and drooling, "Perfect. Don't you need to keep a record of this for taxes? You have a payroll receipt?"

Dexter and John looked at one another. Dexter laughed, "Let's call this an under the table job. Contract work. We pay enough taxes," Dexter said.

"I don't think you'd be a good President. They check tax records for you to run," Nelson said, with a wink.

"Ok, smart ass. Mind your own business, punk. If you want to get paid next time," Dexter said, with a glare.

"I like this kid," John said, giving Nelson a fist bump.

Nelson unhooked his camera lens from the front and gently placed it in the camera bag. He took the wad of cash, unzipped a side compartment and jammed it in. "It works; appreciate the work. Been fun helping you guys get the website into this decade. I think your online sales will skyrocket.

Then we can talk about Facebook ads and other marketing strategies."

John slapped Nelson on the back, knocking him forward. "Let's go slow. With your prices, I'm not sure we can do much other than the website. But, the Facebook page has already helped us sell stuff. You got the touch kid."

"If you guys need help with anything, please call. You have my card. I'll be in touch about the site going live."

"Not so fast. We're keeping you around on contract. Plenty of business for you to do. We finished a pick yesterday and have a bunch of stuff in the warehouse for you to get online. We'll be in touch," Dexter said.

Nelson gave a thumb up. "I need to get to class. I'll catch you guys later. Call me when you're ready to get those items online."

Nelson disappeared behind the glass doors in the front of the shop. Dexter waved John over and pointed down at the newspaper. "You think the kid is telling the truth? Same last name as the racist dude?"

"He's fine," John said.

"We saw him at the Jarrett Stevens rally. His family didn't seem like the minority loving type."

"Same last name, a coincidence," John said.

"All right. But, if the kid is connected to that Darby fella, it is bad for business," Dexter said.

"Not just bad for business. Bad for the soul."

Dexter took one more scan of the newspaper and threw it in the trashcan. "We got bigger fish to fry. We need money. Let's get a pick in."

19.

It was about 10 AM and the morning turned from cool to sticky warm. John pressed down on the gas of the extended full size van, trying to make up time for a late morning pick. The tires screamed down Highway 24, heading west toward Carthage. A light sprinkle of rain brushed across the windshield.

"I hate this weather. It makes my armpits juicy," John said, raising an arm like a chicken flapping its wings.

"You're a disgusting human; you know that, right?" Dexter asked.

John ignored the backhanded compliment and focused on the empty highway. "Where's Samantha sending us?"

"Carthage. Repeat customer," Dexter said, scanning an Excel spreadsheet.

"Did we do well there last time?" John asked, sipping a Diet Cherry Coke.

"According to my records, we did well," Dexter said, tapping the spreadsheet with a pen.

"We need to keep the money train rolling. Carthage the one with the barns filled with classic cars? I think we scored a 63' Ford Falcon convertible, if I remember," John said, scanning the road.

"Nope. You're thinking of the Cooper's place. This is the dude with the tractors. Vintage John Deere variety. He's got 40s, 50s, and 60s models."

John nodded and tapped on his Styrofoam cup. "Need a profitable pick today. More rusty gold to build our new online presence. We need more time to build momentum."

"You think Nelson is helping the biz?" Dexter asked.

"I think so. But, can I be honest? He makes me nervous. He exudes social awkwardness in the shop. And, having the same last name as the town racist? He's got that Opie vibe with something dark underneath. You tracking?"

"I can see it. You're not being fair. He's just a college kid trying to find his way in the world. You were awkward at that age. Remember when your mom had to sew extensions on your sweaters so they'd fit right? Let's not jump to conclusions about Nelson until we know for sure."

"Please don't bring up the growth spurt days. Those are days, of my history, worth forgetting.. You think we need to look into Danny Darby being related to Nelson? Don't need that noise around the shop."

"I think you're paranoid. If he said he's not related, he's not related. There's nothing to suggest he thinks like his folks. Maybe the brainwashing to hate black people hasn't kicked into gear."

Dexter adjusted his trucker hat and pondered the Jarrett Stevens rally. He didn't like the message and brainwashing of people in LeClaire with its history of racism. "LeClaire is not immune to racism. You remember high school when Peter Lewis enrolled senior year? His family was one of the few black families in town. He was treated like a second class citizen."

John nodded and took a deep slurp on his Coke. "Things are different. We have a black President for crying out loud. Our grandparents would turn over in their graves knowing a black man is leading the free world."

"True. But, I remember stories they told about Kansas City in the 60s and 70s. Black families pushed out of their homes when highway 71 was built. Many forced east of the city into slums and ghettos. That is when all the whites fled for the suburbs. Called it "white flight."

John pulled down his sunglasses and smiled, impressed with Dexter's knowledge of black history in Missouri. "Bravo, Dex. I'm impressed. Not just a pretty face."

Dexter punched John in his pudgy arm. "Shut

your hole. This is important. Kansas City is less than two hundred miles from here. These are real people and have problems we don't understand."

"We have problems. I have a mortgage. I am still looking for a girl to share the John-love with. I get gassy after Chinese food. I got all kinds of problems."

"You're an idiot. That's the problem with us."

"Who are us?" John asked.

"White people."

"Are you considered white being Irish and all?"

"My family is Irish, but born here. I think white is accurate."

John placed his Coke into the cup holder in the center console of the van. He gripped the steering wheel with both hands. "You think white folks have it better than others?"

"Sometimes. Not always because of skin color. But, I think there are people who have opportunities and some who don't, because of their ethnicity."

"Wow, Dex. I never knew you cared about this stuff."

"Not only a pretty face, remember? I think about things. Not just finding antiques and the next trip to the lake."

"Well, renaissance man. Let's put the black history conversation on hold for now. We need to make money."

20.

Dexter stood on the wraparound porch waiting for the owner to answer the door. A gust of wind blew dust and debris from the porch. He yanked his phone from his pocket and texted Samantha to confirm the picking address.

Confirmed.

A large and sweaty tattooed man opened the broken screen door and gave the guys a look over. He then moved a cigarette dangling from his mouth, to the right, and smiled through blackened teeth, "You from Antique Adventures? 'Bout time you showed up. "

"Yes, sir. Sorry for being late. My partner drives like a grandma," Dexter said, giving John a stare and handing the sweaty man a paper flyer. "These are the items we're looking for. Think you can help?"

The man scanned the flyer and handed it back to Dexter, "I don't read so well. What you see in the yard is the shit I got. If you want some of it, make me an offer. No funny stuff," he said, scratching an arm pit.

John gave a half smile and turned to face about five acres of rusted cars, signs, barns, sheds, out-houses, and other piles of rusty gold. "Sounds fantastic, sir. A lot of potential in your yard," John said, reaching out a hand.

The man gave him a puzzled look, like shaking hands was a foreign cultural norm.

John's hand dangled.

The man tossed the half-smoked cigarette on the ground, and reached for another, from a stained plaid shirt front pocket. "My family has lived here all my life. All that rust in the yard is a piece of our history."

Most people who sell items to Antique Adventures have an unhealthy attachment to their "rusty history." That can be a good thing, or bad. Good when they'll let it go and acknowledge their hoarding tendencies. Bad when the emotional attachment is too strong, leaving the boys unable to make a deal worth the gas money spent for the trip. Dexter was nervous this might be an emotional seller.

"You care where we start?" Dexter asked, taking in the view of the yard.

The man pointed to a red barn in the distance, a hundred yards from the house. "You can start in that their barn. There's shit in there. I'll get the keys."

Dexter and John gave the proverbial this might be good nod and waited for the man to return.

"You all right about this one?" John asked.

"Hard to tell. Guess that's why we're called Antique Adventures. Adventure every time," Dexter said, with a wink.

"I hope he's got another John Deere tractor. We made ten grand on the last one."

"Not going to happen. Golden rule: 'lucky once, never twice'."

"Come on, Dex. Have a little faith. We've scored with repeat customers."

"Not on the same items."

"True," John said, kicking up dirt on the ground.

"I don't have a good vibe about this guy."

"Why? Because he's sweaty and wears a shirt, that's not been washed... ever."

Dexter chuckled, "No. I saw a swastika on his left forearm."

"Are you going to give me another lecture on race?"

"No. I don't like what the Nazis represented. They were sick dudes."

"Agreed. Old tattoo and he's changed his ways, possibly?"

"These old, white, backwoods folks don't change. Their ideologies are sealed in cement. Not going to teach these dogs new tricks. If you know what I mean."

John tossed his finished Coke in a barrel on the

side of the yard. "I don't care if he's a racist. I want to make money off his rusty gold. He can be white, black, tall, short, or a Martian, and I'll buy his junk for the right price. If it makes money."

"You're so simple minded."

"Nope. Just a smart business man. You can't be picky when making money."

The sweaty man came back to the front of the house and limped up to the men. "I got the keys. Let's see what I can do for you."

John rubbed his hands together and smiled at the man, and Dexter said, "Yes, sir. Let's get into it and see what kind of deals we can make."

The men stood in front of a red barn with white trim.

John and Dexter pulled leather gloves from their belts and yanked them tight. The man fiddled with the rusty pad lock and cursed under his breath. Dexter nodded at John, trying to get him to inspect the tattoo. He mouthed, "I told you."

John wagged his head side to side and ignored Dexter and the tattoo. The doors of the red barn squealed open and a plume of dust covered the men. Dexter wiped his eyes and tee shirt. "Dusty in here. What we like to see. The dustier, the older, the older, the better, I always say."

The sweaty man sucked on his cigarette and limped to the right side of the barn. He situated a metal folding chair, "I will sit over here. Holler if you have questions about my stuff. Going to rest my eyes," he said, leaning back in the chair, his belly sliding over his leather belt buckle.

Dexter and John nodded and made their way to the center of the barn. Dexter went right and John left. The strategy of a larger barn is to work from the center to the edges. You don't want to miss anything of value. A lot of times the larger and more valuable items like cars and tractors are in the center of the room.

John glided up and down rows of tools, jars filled with nails, and rusted out bicycles on the walls. He poked and turned over two items. Nothing catching his eye.

John knelt down to peek into a cardboard box that had brown water stains. He opened the damp flaps on the top and stuck his head in.

A neat pile of white garments lay inside the box. John undid the cotton material and allowed them to unravel to the dusty floor. He examined the mystery fabrics.

The fabric had a cut in the neck line and a red cross on the right lapel. It appeared to have a blood stain in the center of the robe. John placed the garment aside and kept digging deeper into the box.

John raised a pointed triangular hat from the bottom of the box. He turned it over and noticed two eye holes cut into the front of a hood hanging from the back.

Standard Ku Klux Klan issue.

21.

John waved Dexter over and tried not to alert the large sweaty man dozing off in his chair. Dexter nodded and ignored the wave. John swung his arms side to side and pointed at the box on the floor.

Dexter placed a small lamp back on a shelf and glided over to meet him.

"What is it tubby? Find a Mona Lisa?"

"No time for fat jokes. Look in the box," John said, pointing at the crumpled cardboard.

Dexter leaned over, scanned the contents, and shrugged his shoulders, not knowing what he was looking at. John unraveled the white robe and held it in front of Dexter, pointing to the symbol. "Look familiar?"

Dexter touched the garment like it would reveal its origins, "Is it Catholic?"

"Not even close. I didn't know what it was until

I saw this...," John said, holding up the pointy hat and placing it over his sweaty forehead. "Now?"

Dexter leapt back and acted as if stung by a bee. "Holy shit. Those are KKK digs. You think sweaty guy is in the Klan?" Dexter asked, glancing at sweaty guy, snoring in a metal folding chair.

"Maybe. But, I hate this stuff."

"I didn't think you cared about racism?" Dexter asked.

"I never said I didn't care. I just don't see myself as a racist and don't think about it all that much."

"If we're honest, I think everyone is a racist. Thinks their culture is superior to others. It's not only the KKK," Dexter said, kneeling down to look further into the box.

"Don't need a lecture. We got to leave."

Dexter pulled out a glass frame and dusted off the front. He scanned the picture and scratched his head. "I think we found our answer," Dexter said, pointing to a tall man in the photo.

John glanced at the picture and then looked over to the sweaty man in the chair. He stared back at the frame and pointed at the man, "He's a little younger and slimmer in the picture. Confident it's him."

"You never know who you'll run into on a pick, huh?" Dexter said, punching John in the arm.

John wiped his eye and placed the hood and robe back into the box. "You crying?" Dexter asked.

"No. I got dust in my eye."

Dexter didn't believe his response and lifted his chubby chin in his hand, "Those are tears. Is this KKK stuff bothering you?"

"Yeah, a little. I don't understand how people can hate others, so much. Groups like that are disgusting and need to be wiped from the earth. We need to leave."

Dexter slapped John on the back and wrapped an arm around his thick body, "I thought you didn't care if someone was a racist. It's all about making money. Get conflicted when it involves the Klan, huh? This is a big day for us. We should celebrate with a huge Diet Cherry Coke. You in?"

"I don't care. I want to get out of this place. This guy doesn't deserve our business."

Dexter closed up the box and slid it under a rusty desk. He dusted off his jeans and looked over at John, pausing in his tracks.

The sweaty man stood in front of the metal chair."Who you calling disgusting, son?" asked the man.

John stumbled over his words and tried to pass it over to Dexter. "He didn't mean it. He just says things; it wasn't about you," Dexter said.

"I don't like no punks coming to my place and calling me names. You find something that made you call me names?" the sweaty man asked.

John peeked over at the cardboard box on the floor and played dumb, "Nope. I had my eye on some old lamps. Nothing else."

The sweaty man pushed the men apart like parting the Red Sea and headed for the cardboard box. He leaned over to pull the box from under the desk, flipped the edges of the box open, and peeked inside. He held up the white robe like a trophy. "Oh, yeah. This brings me back to when I was not much older than you guys. A long time ago," he said, scratching his chin and smiling.

John stood back, folded his arms and tried not to explode with rage. He couldn't believe a person could speak casually about a hate group like the KKK. He crept forward as the sweaty man beamed, looking at the contents in the box. "In a past life, I'd beat the shit out of you guys for talking trash. I detect some kind of accent on this one," he said, nodding at Dexter.

"I'm Irish. But, I doubt you hear an accent. Born and raised in LeClaire. That's Midwest you hear."

"I can spot a foreigner a mile away," the sweaty man said.

John crept in and stood in front of the man. He stared into his wrinkled eyes and placed a finger in the center of his chest. "Don't talk to him like that. The O'Kane family means more to LeClaire, Missouri than any of your racist friends. I don't know what you've done in your past. But, I hope God is merciful on your soul," John said, his face blushing red.

The man put up his hands in surrender and took a slow step backwards. He threw the robe on the desk, "I don't want any trouble. But, those racist bastards are still alive and well. I can make a call and you boys will disappear from God's green earth," he said, revealing only a handful of teeth.

Dexter came up behind John and the man and pulled his Beretta from the back of his jeans. He pointed the barrel at the back of the man's head and whispered in his ear, "You might think we're just two local pickers. But, you do not understand who we are, and what we can do. We know people too."

The man held his hands straight in the air, displaying a hole in the armpit of his shirt, "Easy, Irish boy. Let's call it even. You leave now and forget this ever happened."

Dexter gripped the Beretta M92 tighter and pressed it further into his head, "We will leave now. Never to come back," Dexter said, sliding away from the frozen sweaty man, holding the gun between his eyes, "How rude... I never caught your name."

The sweaty man swallowed, blinked hard, and snarled out his name, "Darby. Reggie Darby."

22.

Dexter and John sat silently, each waiting for the other to speak, as highway noise hummed in the background. They headed back to Antique Adventures having decided business with the KKK was a conflict of interest. At least, it was a conflict with their own ideals of how people should be treated.

Dexter broke the ice.

"You don't think the sweaty KKK guy is related to Nelson?" he asked.

"Duh, of course, he is. The entire family is a bunch of racist loons. They probably had Thanksgiving dinner last November. Talked justification of the white man slaughtering Indians. We need to fire Nelson when we get back."

Dexter palmed John in the face and focused back on the highway. He couldn't believe what he was hearing, "Easy... chunky. Let's not jump to any conclusions about Nelson. Their family may be a bunch of racist idiots. But, Mr. Pointy hat might be a mere coincidence. Nelson's a smart kid and we need him for the business. Not to mention, we made no money off the KKK warlord today. We need the online biz to make it up," he said, dropping a wad of tobacco in his lip.

"You still dipping?"

"When I'm stressed. I think the last time was when I picked up my dad from prison. Took more than one pinch that year."

"You ever think about him?"

"Once in a while. Wonder what it would be like to have him around for my kids. That's all."

John nodded.

"Oh, yeah... forgot I was mad at you. Are you shitting me? You want someone associated with the KKK around the shop? I don't want my name, your name, or Antique Adventures affiliated with those dirt bags. A risk we don't need. We are a small business and bad press could shut us down."

Dexter nodded and turned down the Royals game on the radio. He gave a grin, "I could be wrong, but, when people are confronted with racists, their tune changes. A few hours ago you seemed neutral about the issue. Now you care. Sweaty KKK dude messed up your head," Dexter said.

"Don't know if your diagnosis is right Doctor Phil. But, the KKK dude made me sick to my stomach. If that is being confronted with racism, so be it. I don't want to be around it. Hard to think those people still exist today," John said, rubbing his temple.

Dexter stared down the empty Missouri highway and watched the sun disappear behind a far off hill. A mixture of satisfaction and confusion settled in his mind. John contemplating the atrocities of racism was encouraging. It was an issue most comfortable, middle-class, white men, living in small Midwest towns, don't think about often. Could it be the way the O'Kane's were treated when they immigrated to America in the 50s? Called Green Niggers, Carrot-Tops, and Potato Breath. Dexter had never enjoyed being the only Irish kid in school.

Dexter found solace in knowing everybody must deal with their own racial bias. No one was indifferent on the issue because everyone has a story. The struggles of the O'Kanes, while not being comparable to the black community in Kansas City only a few decades back, made Dexter sensitive to the issue. People needed to think through the ramifications of racism, even if we live in a world naïve enough to believe racism ended after Abraham Lincoln, Martin Luther King, and now, the first black President Barack Obama.

"I'm proud of you big fella. You're finally putting on your man-pants and thinking about things that matter. Not just where you'll get your next taco and when DefCon4 will come out," Dexter said, with an evil grin.

"Let's not get crazy. I still need my tacos and video games. It's how I relax. I want Nelson out of the business. If I see the sweaty KKK guy again, I'm not sure what I'll do," John said, wiping sweat from his brow.

Dexter flipped on his blinker as the Antique Adventures van veered off the dark highway. He sat quiet for a beat and reflected on John's response about firing Nelson. "I know the Darby name doesn't look good. But, I want to keep Nelson. At least for contract work. He's doing an excellent job and, so far, hasn't hurting anyone. Let's give it a few more days, and we'll revisit. Deal?" Dexter asked, raising a hand for a high five.

John glanced down in his lap. He didn't like Dexter's suggestion but he was done fighting for the day. His stomach was gurgling and nothing would divert his attention away from meeting that primal need. "I'm tired. I don't care. Do what you think is best for the business," John said, tapping on the passenger window, "I need some tacos."

A bright red and yellow sign taco lit up the sky in downtown LeClaire, Missouri. Pancho's. The best tacos this side of the state.

Dexter veered into the crowded parking lot, found a parking spot, and before the car was turned off, John leapt from the passenger seat to the pavement. Dexter shook his head, "You must be hungry tubby," he said, killing the engine.

"All this racism talk has made me hungry. I may be naïve to the history of the black community, but, I do know one thing. These Mexicans can cook the shit out of a taco," John said, with a toothy grin.

23.

The First Baptist Church of LeClaire was a white steepled building on the corner of Hillcrest Avenue and Main Street. It was founded a couple years after the Civil War by a group of farmers who were trying to make a life for themselves in LeClaire. At one time, FBC LeClaire had over three hundred members, which was large for a town of a thousand in 1870. Now, in a town of 20,000, the church was lucky to get seventy-five on a Sunday.

The Darby's squeezed into their pews ten minutes late. Nelson and Danny had argued over bathroom time, just like old times. Mrs. Darby gave each boy, now men, a piercing glance as if to tell them to shut up or get out.

A pastor climbed the steps at the right side of the small stage. He waved a paper fan across his wide face. "Welcome to First Baptist LeClaire. If you're visiting this Lord's Day, glad you chose to worship with us. We don't believe in perfect people. Only a perfect God," the pastor said, pulling out a white handkerchief and wiping his balding head.

Danny glanced around the church looking for single girls who wanted to be naughty for a night. No luck. The church was filled with middle-aged and older senior saints waiting to meet Jesus face to face. He played with his black boots, draped across his lap, blocking out the pastor's voice.

Nelson listened, his interest fading in and out. There was a time when Pastor Smith's sermons were interesting. A time when he had dreamed of the Biblical worlds in far off lands. The vision and hope of the Bible still captured his imagination at times. But, the Darby's didn't attend church much after Danny went to prison. This morning Nelson was distracted.

"This morning it brings me a great deal of grief to share the next prayer request," the pastor said. Nelson perked up.

"Last night, a young black man, Larry Woods, was severely beaten outside Chelly's Mexican restaurant."

Their father nudged Danny in the ribcage and gave him a smile. He whispered in his ear, "We got that swamp monkey," he said, in a seething tone.

Nelson shifted in the hard wooden pew and tried to focus on the words of the pastor, not knowing what his father was saying to Danny, "It is times like these we must pull together as a church community. We must fight against the injustices of our broken world. It is at times like these we must pray, encourage, and help one another."

Nelson nodded his head with passion and imagined the pastor was Martin Luther King giving his I Have a Dream speech at the Washington Memorial in 1963. He knew deep in his bones what Danny and Rick did was wrong. The rallies of Jarrett Stevens were not what this country stood for. But there was resistance.

Danny stood up in his pew and waved a hand at the pastor as he continued to speak. "Boo! Boo! What if the black dude had it coming? Do we still stand up for him?"

Mrs. Darby slugged Danny in the side and he recoiled, looking down at her, "What ma?"

She whispered, turning red, "Sit down right now. You are embarrassing the family," she said, clenching her teeth.

"This pastor has no right to say all this stuff. I don't think we need to protect everybody. Some people need to vanish from the earth. We know who they are," he said, glancing down at the pew.

Mrs. Darby placed a hand over her forehead and glanced down the row, all eyes directed at their pew. Danny continued, "I think not everyone was created equal. There are inferior people on the planet and they need to be done away with."

The pastor tried to gain his composure and squinted through the lights, trying to see Danny standing in the back of the chapel. "I'm not sure who's talking. But, I think what you are saying is offensive to God, and to me. In God's eyes, everyone was created equal, and in his image. All of God's creation are precious to him," he said, still trying to find the source of the voice in the back of the church.

"Bunch of horse shit," said Danny, the congregation gasping in unison with his profanity laced rant.

"Please son, don't curse in God's house. It's unnecessary."

Danny ignored the pleas of his mother, and now father, to sit down and shut up. He raised his fists and his face turned bright red like a balloon ready to explode. "I'm so tired of your hypocrisy. You come to church on Sunday and on Monday you tell your racist jokes at the office, in the bars, and your basements. Acting all holier-than-thou when deep down you are just like me. People of real faith that believe in the real gospel. A gospel where the weak are destroyed and the superior race reigns supreme."

A black man sat peacefully in the last pew of the church and observed Danny and the pastor's dialogue. He folded his hands and shook his head side to side, almost as if listening to Bach on the radio. He took off a brown top hat and placed it on the pew bench. Next, he gripped the pew in front of him with frail hands and wobbled as he rose to his feet. He glided over to Danny, who did not see the man coming up behind him. He placed a hand on his shoulder, "You're afraid, son. This angry tirade is coming from a bad place. A place of hurt," the black man said, in a smooth and calm manner.

24.

D anny glanced to his right to see who was touching his shoulder and almost didn't notice the man standing next to him. The pastor had now left the stage and was moving toward the back of the church to meet Danny. From the right aisle, the pastor saw Danny looking at the black man now touching his shoulder.

"You better remove your disgusting black hand from my shoulder before I rip it off," Danny said, with spit bubbling up in the corner of his mouth.

The black man smiled, with a calm look, as if there were not a care in the world. As if he'd seen this situation played out multiple times in his seventy years of life. He patted Danny's back, and he recoiled, "I used to be angry like you. Didn't understand how people could speak poorly of one another. Kids in school called me nigger, swamp monkey, and slave, because of my skin color. I hurt no one, but... "Danny stepped back trying to disengage from the calm speech of the man, "I don't need no sob story old man," Danny said.

"You didn't let me finish, son. I used to be angry. But, I'm not anymore. Realized it wasn't other people who were the problem. I was the problem. You kind of live your life oblivious to the pains, hurts, and struggles of others. I don't pretend that using hurtful words toward other races is right, it's not. But, I was just as guilty. I became angry and made judgments toward whites, and all races. That wasn't right."

Nelson sat underneath the conversation and smiled. He could tell Danny was softening, maybe in an incremental way. The calming words of the man were penetrating Danny's soul and his face had turned back to its normal pasty white.

The pastor arrived on the scene and stood behind the black man. "Is everything okay here?" he asked, wiping sweat off his forehead.

"Oh, Pastor Smith, everything is just fine. There's a misunderstanding here with..." the black man held out his hand for a shake, "I'm rude, young man. My name is Lester Banks, what's yours?" he asked.

Danny stared at the pastor and Lester and didn't know what to say. He knew on one level everything he said about hurt and anger was true. Danny's childhood had been filled with consternation because of his small stature, delayed puberty, and having lived in a racist family where his dad was not home because of long hours, and his participation in Jarrett Stevens rallies. The hurt ran deep.

Danny laid out a dead fish handshake to Lester and didn't make eye contact. He snapped out of his reflection on what Lester said and his childhood and felt the rage bubble over again. "Screw this shit. I'm getting out of this place," Danny said, knocking the pastor and Lester back like bowling pins.

Nelson and the rest of his family watched Danny slam open the back church doors. They felt the eyes of the congregation beaming into their backs. Rick waved at the family and, embarrassed, they slid out of the pews, with heads down, and scurried through the back doors of the church behind Danny.

Nelson held back for a second and shook Lester's hand, "I appreciated what you said. It resonated with me. Even with my crazy family," he said, as Lester smiled back.

"Good to hear, son. Hope it makes difference with your brother some day. Life is too short to be angry," Lester said.

Nelson nodded and turned to the pastor to shake his hand, "Sorry about all this. My family is crazy. Keep up the shepherding work pastor," he said, with an awkward half smile.

"Come back anytime. We are all a little crazy. They let me be a pastor which proves the point," the pastor said, wiping his face, and forcing a smile.

Nelson paused and stared at the pastor like he said he had two heads. He couldn't even understand why his racist family would be invited to church after what Danny did and said. Before Nelson could respond, the pastor said, with a grin, "That's how grace works"

25.

D anny took a hit on his cigarette and fumbled with his phone on the porch of his house. He scrolled through the contacts and found Jarrett Stevens.

"Jarrett. It's Danny. Can we talk?"

The smooth talking Stevens perked up on the other line; they'd known each other for some time. "How are things, son? Glad to hear you are out of Leavenworth."

Danny ignored the comment; he didn't want to relive the hell he'd paid for roughing up that black kid. He gave a half smile and knew not all was lost in prison. "Thanks for the work inside. It saved my life. I don't know if I'd have made the five years without it."

There was a pause on the phone as Stevens planned his words, "That's what American Renaissance is all about. We are purifying the human race of the rabble and rubbish that makes our communities unsafe and trashy. I'm only here to help our disciples. How can I help you today?"

The cigarette laid on the edge of the railing on the front porch and Danny reached for it and took a deep drag. He blew it out, "I have a situation."

"What kind of situation?"

"It happened at church. A black dude was trying to be nice and stuff."

"Well, Danny. Many of these people are phony and don't care about others. A front to get hand-outs most of time. Tell me more."

"He seemed all right. I don't think he was trying to get nothing from me," Danny said, tossing the cigarette on the lawn below.

"Deception of the Enemy. He wants us to believe those low class people are safe. They are on our side. But, they aren't. They want to destroy our communities and take advantage of the systems we have in place. What happened that has you concerned?"

"I kind of said stuff at church. The pastor was blabbing on about people being equal. I didn't agree, gave him a piece of my mind."

"You talked during the sermon?"

"Yep. I told him I think some people are inferior and not equal in God's eyes."

There was a pause of a couple beats; Stevens was surprised by what Danny did. "Wow. Brave of you, son. In the future, think before you speak. I'm proud of you, nonetheless."

"But..."

"But, what?"

"This black guy told me I was angry. He wasn't even angry over what I said. I don't understand."

"Hmmm... well, many blacks are conditioned to not feel pain. He's been brainwashed by the church not to acknowledge his inferiority. A coping mechanism."

Danny nodded and listened to the advice of Stevens. "I'm just having a hard time. No one has ever responded like that. They usually want to beat my brains in."

"I'd find a different church. A church where the pure gospel of the superior race is preached. I'll ask around."

"I don't think most people in our parent's church know half of what we believe. Touchy subject. Besides, we don't go all that much."

"Well, son most people are unenlightened and don't understand the ramifications of their wayward thinking. Our organization exists to set the minds and hearts of people straight in America. A noble cause. One I'm glad you're part of."

Danny paced the porch and something switched off inside. He pounded a post holding up the front of the house and kicked over a rocking chair on the left side of the porch. "I want that black guy dead."

"What?"

"You heard me. I want that smiley faced swamp monkey, talking about how angry I am, dead. He has no right to tell me who I am. He doesn't know the shit I've been through. He needs to die. What can I do?"

Silence.

Stevens spoke in hushed tone. "If you think this man is a threat, we can make arrangements for his departure. That's why American Renaissance exists. You want to proceed?"

Danny was now on the front lawn and his pacing sped up as he ripped another cigarette from his flannel shirt pocket. The cigarette dangled from the side of his mouth as he spoke, "Yes, hell yes. I want that black son of a bitch dead. He doesn't deserve to breathe the air I breathe," Danny said, coughing through his last puff on the cigarette.

"Your wish is my command. Consider it done. I will call later and make arrangements. I'm seeing real progress in you Danny."

Danny nodded and hung up the phone. He kept hearing Lester in his ear, "I used to be angry like you..."

26.

The next morning, John dusted the top shelf of antique guns from the Civil War era. He climbed down the ladder and tossed the rag at Dexter. "How'd we do last pick?"

Dexter gave a thumbs up and tapped on the keyboard of the computer. The boys found two items that had surprised even them. A vase from the early 19th century they were confident was a remake turned out to be an original. And, the front end of a 1936 Ford pickup was a goldmine. A collector in Nebraska needed the front to complete a project and had paid top dollar.

"The vase and Ford front end are paying out. Not to mention the new website and the images Nelson posted are bringing in all kinds of new customers."

John wiped sweat from his brow and wiggled his sagging jeans. "He's not bad. But, I still have my reservations. His family seems creepy."

"Who cares? All of our families are creepy. Have you met your mother?"

John smirked, "She's got issues. I don't want the shop wrapped up in some racist agenda crap. That could bring us down. I don't want to find another job."

Dexter slapped on the keypad and then glanced up at John with a smile. "We won't let it get that far. Besides, we don't know if there is a real concern. It might just be a coincidence he's related to some bad people. You want me to talk with him today?"

John looked at his watch, "Yeah. I think he'll be in soon."

Before John could say another word, the glass doors of the shop swung open. Nelson waddled into the store and flung a backpack in the corner of his makeshift cubicle. He raised a hand at the boys. "How are we today?"

Dexter came over next to his small desk and placed a hand on his shoulder. "You're a gold-mine."

"Why's that?"

"We are killing it online. All because of your pretty pictures."

Nelson nodded and gave a toothy grin, "Good to hear. I'm telling you, the web is where it's at. You needed to get that website out of the 90's and I knew it would profit."

Dexter slapped him on the back and glided to the other side of the store. The wind from the opened glass door hit Nelson as he peaked up from his desk. A mailman sauntered in and tossed a newspaper on the counter at the back of the shop.

"You guys hear about the crazy shit that happened last night?"

Dexter and John leaned over the LeClaire Gazette and glanced down. The headline read:

Black Man Slain on Front Lawn

The boys looked at one another and shook their heads. Nelson stumbled from behind his makeshift desk and came over to the paper.

"What's up? You guys look sad."

Nelson mumbled through the headline and raised the newspaper to read the story.

Lester Banks was strung up on his front porch last night. No eyewitnesses and no evidence, yet.

Nelson scratched his head as the name sounded familiar in his ear. He flipped to a back page and his mouth opened, "I've met this guy. He was at our church a couple days ago. My brother and he exchanged words."

Dexter asked, "Your brother do this?"

Nelson shook his head. "I don't think so. He was at home last night, I think. But, the exchange in the church was not pretty."

John butted in, "Did the man threaten your brother?"

"No, the other way around. Danny was yelling at the pastor because of what he was saying. Stuff about people being created equal. He didn't like it.

Lester, I think was his name, told my brother he was angry. Danny didn't like that so much. Flew off the handle and stormed out of church."

Nelson backed away from the paper and acted as if it would explode. He ran to his desk, grabbed his backpack, and waved to the guys. "I need to go. Catch you guys tomorrow."

Nelson disappeared from the shop and the boys were shaking their heads in shock. "If this kid's brother is involved, I think he needs to find other work. We can't have this around the shop. Bad for business," John said, sipping on a Diet Cherry Coke.

Dexter nodded, "Hope there's no connection. Nobody wants to be part of something that dark. I'll let things cool off and call him later."

Dexter slid behind the counter and plopped into a chair behind a computer. "Don't want to lose that kid. I'm liking the numbers on the screen."

27.

"You should've seen that old guy. He was shaking like a leaf and begging for mercy," Danny said, passing a joint to the rest of his crew.

Nelson leaned against the door of the bedroom and scanned the hallway, not sure what to think. His mother glided down the hall and gave Nelson a raised eyebrow. "Why are you standing by Danny's room? He's got friends over."

Nelson nodded and shrugged. "I heard pounding on the wall. Wanted to check it out."

"You know those boys are rough. Leave them be; it's nothing," she said, disappearing to the front of the house.

Danny said, "It felt so good. Like some kind of revenge at play. That swamp monkey deserved every lick."

Nelson swung the bedroom door open and pointed a finger at Danny. The crew held up hands and waved the marijuana smoke from the haze covering the middle of the room. "You did it!" Nelson shouted.

A small man smiled and took another hit on the joint just passed in his direction, "What are you talking 'bout kid? Who invited you in here?"

Danny elbowed the man and ripped the joint from his hand, taking a drag. "It's my kid brother. He's no harm. Can we help you?"

Nelson leaned over Danny and pointed a finger at his forehead. "You killed Lester Banks. The man in the church. You did it, you bastard."

Danny held up his hands in surrender, "What you smoking kid? You getting secondhand smoke from my room? I ain't kill nobody," Danny said, as laughs grew around the circle.

"I heard you. You said it felt so good. What? Tell me now."

"Careful what you say, bro. You don't know what you're talking about. I remember a time when you'd be affirming the situation."

"What do you mean?"

"You're changing, kid. Too bad. It was worth every hit."

"Who did you hurt? Was it Lester Banks?"

"I don't kill and tell. Why do you care? You going to tell on me?" Danny said, with a smile looking for affirmation from the crew.

"If I'm sleeping next to a murderer, I will say something."

Danny rose to his feet, got near Nelson and blew smoke in his face. "I ain't kill that monkey from the church. He's not worth my time. He'll be dead before long. Don't be coming round here and accusing me of nothing. I don't appreciate it. You need to respect your elders," Danny said, tapping on Nelson's chest.

Nelson back peddled and wiped the smoke from around his face and tried to speak. "You swear? I don't want you going back to jail."

"Swear. I will not go to jail. Keep to your own business and everything will be fine."

Nelson turned to leave the room and paused before crossing the threshold. "I agree with Lester. You are an angry man. But, you don't have to be. Be careful before it bites you. The next time you might never come home from jail."

Danny shoved Nelson out into the hallway and slammed the door. "Worry about yourself. If I'm angry, it's justified."

28.

Nelson slid a two weeks resignation note to Dexter and John in a booth at Rudy's diner. Dexter sipped a black coffee and John downed a Cherry Coke.

"You want a milkshake? Best in LeClaire," Dexter said.

"Can't. Lactose intolerant," Nelson said, with a frown.

"That sucks. What's this?" Dexter asked, glancing at the handwritten note.

"My two weeks."

"You're quitting? Why?"

"You might be right about my family. Stuff going down I'm not comfortable with. Best we part ways. Can't bring that drama around the shop."

"What do you know?"

"Not much. Brother is the same guy who went to prison. Violent. He told me to stay out of it. But, I think he's lying. I can tell."

John picked at a mound of pancakes and scanned the letter. "I live by a simple principle. Innocent until proven guilty. Your brother could be telling the truth. Or, not. Your family has some crazy beliefs. We'd hate to see you go. Do what you got to do," John said, with an indifferent tone.

Nelson nibbled on a piece of bacon and shook his head. "I love working with you guys. You're different. But, I don't want to put AA in a bad spot because of my crazy family. You understand, right?"

"I've been pulling for you the last couple of months. My partner and I think you do great work. Our business is growing because of you. But, we don't want to compromise our integrity if your family is up to something shady," Dexter said, steam from his coffee wafting into his unshaven face.

Nelson nodded. "I appreciate it. This is like the first real job I've ever had. It beats the hell out of fast food. I just wish someone could help me. I feel alone."

"What kind of help?" Dexter asked.

"Ugh, like, detective work, without a real detective. I need someone to follow my brother and see what he is up to. I don't think he's telling the truth."

Dexter and John glanced at one another and smiled at Nelson. "We know a couple guys for these situations," Dexter said.

Nelson laughed and wiped the corner of his mouth with a napkin. "Who? You're a couple of hicks running an antique shop," Nelson said, looking around the restaurant.

"Easy, kid. There are other sides to the ordinariness of these hicks. We run a side business that might help."

"A side business? What? Like those guys hired to find dudes cheating on their wives?"

"Not exactly. We are more like an underground justice society. When the normal channels of public service aren't helpful, we step in."

Nelson looked at Dexter and then at John. He gave a wide toothy grin and sipped his milk. "You're like hit men? I'm not buying it. Give me proof."

Dexter slid a card across the table. Nelson read the front and mumbled the words. "You know the Chief of Police in LeClaire? Not a big deal. You could've donated money to the department, and he gave you a card. Anyone can get one of these."

"Look at it closer. Read the back."

"Personal cell phone. Okay, what does that prove?"

"How many Police Chiefs give out their personal number?"

"Maybe it's significant. You don't have the look."

"What kind of look?"

"I imagine someone other than two dudes driving trucks and picking rusty gold. Nicer suits and better hair."

Dexter and John laughed. "We live in small town Missouri. We'd stick out like a sore thumb."

"How do you help the Police Chief?"

"You remember the last Chief? The one who died a few years ago?"

"I think so."

"We found his killer."

"No way. How come I never heard it on the news?"

"We don't use normal channels of justice. Our goal is not to be seen or heard. So please keep your mouth shut about all of this," Dexter said, with a wink.

"You know how to shoot a gun?" Nelson asked.

"Dex served as a Navy Seal before blowing out a knee," John said, his face animated.

"That was a long time ago. But, yes, I can handle a gun just fine."

Nelson nodded, still not convinced of their resume.

The waitress came to the table to refill the coffees, Coke, and milk. She slammed the bill on the table, "How's your family Dexter?"

Dexter saluted his John Deere hat, "Great, Mable. Thanks for asking."

"It was a damn shame about Samantha's brother. He was a good kid," she said, disappearing to the back of the diner with a wad of cash.

Nelson butted in. "What happened to your wife's brother?"

Dexter twirled a spoon at a piece of ice in his coffee to cool it down. He sipped, "Murdered. Same guy, who killed the Chief, killed my bother in law."

Nelson nodded and warmed up to idea that Dexter and John might be of some help. "This is sounding like a real side gig. How can you help?"

"Depends on what you're looking for," John said.

"Danny might've killed Lester Banks. If he did, there will be more trouble down the road. Is that part of your services?"

Dexter wiped his brow and adjusted his hat. "A tall order. We aren't FBI. But, if we find Danny wrapped up dark shit, we'll make sure he's stopped. Will that work?"

Nelson nodded. "What can I do?"

"Stay out of the way. I don't need you hurt on our watch. And don't talk about this conversation. We don't want to blow our cover. Known as antique collectors and nothing else. Got it?"

"Yes, sir. Am I still working at AA?"

"At least another day," Dexter said, with a wink.

29.

An old black woman rocked on the porch of her run down house. She knitted a sweater and glanced up as the Antique Adventures truck pulled into the driveway.

She smiled and gave a wave as if she'd known Dexter and John for years.

"Beautiful day ain't it, boys? Rarely get this cool of weather in July. Thought I'd knit a sweater for my niece. She's always complaining about Missouri winters. Don't blame her."

Dexter peaked at John, confused by the woman who had just lost her husband. She seemed happy for a person who had watched Lester Banks swing from a rope on the front porch.

Dexter took off his John Deere hat and jammed it into his back pocket and glided up the steps to the porch, "Morning, ma'am. Name's Dexter, and this is my partner, John."

The woman gave a look over and lowered her black-rimmed glasses, "You boys ain't gay, are ya?"

Dexter chuckled and shook his head. "Not that I know of. Happily married, three kids. Can't speak for tubby," Dexter said, slapping John's butt.

John rolled his eyes. "You'd be lucky to have a guy like me," he mumbled under his breath.

The woman said, "Times been changing. Seen more gay folks around LeClaire than in my entire seventy seven years. Not that there's anything wrong with it. The good Lord called me to love all people. Even if you don't understand them."

"Dexter's not my type anyhow," John said, sipping a Cherry Coke.

"What can I do for you boys? Haven't seen you round these parts."

Dexter pointed at a couple rusted chairs on the porch and sat down next to the woman. John followed. "We live on the other side of town. First, I want to say I'm sorry about the loss of your husband, Lester was it?"

She set her knitting on a side table and lowered her glasses. A tear welled up in her eye as she folded her hands. "Lester wasn't no perfect man. We had many years of hard times. Fighting, unemployment, and he liked the bottle. An angry man for many years. But, the Lord saw us through. He changed Lester into the sweetest man you'd ever meet. Last ten years were some of our best."

"You must be a tough cookie to hang in there

so many years. How many years you two lovebirds married?" Dexter asked.

"Fifty nine years. Almost made sixty. Got married when I was eighteen. Oh, how young we were, but so in love. He got shipped off to fight in Korea after the honeymoon. Hard first years. How long have you been married?"

"Well, five years to my first wife, Lisa. Five years to my wife, Samantha."

"So many young people getting divorced these days," she said, with a frown.

Dexter laughed and glanced at John who was falling asleep in the chair. "No divorce. My first wife and son were killed in a car accident. Samantha and I met shortly after. I guess the good Lord worked it out," Dexter said, with a grin.

Countenance of the woman changed, and she reached a limp hand toward Dexter and placed it over his. "I'm sorry, son. Very rude of me. Please accept my apology. I guess we have something in common."

Dexter nodded and didn't expect a tear to form in his eye. He wiped it away, "No problem. You didn't know," Dexter said, pulling on police tape flapping in the wind around a pole on the porch. "Don't want to waste your time this morning. Can we ask you a few questions about Lester?"

"You boys police? I've had more police in and out of this house in the last couple days than I can handle."

"No, we aren't police. Your husband was friends with a friend of ours. We wanted to make sure you were doing okay. He's broken up over Lester's death and didn't want to talk. Emotions are raw. So he sent us on his behalf," Dexter said.

The woman gripped Dexter's hand tighter and smiled, "Sweet of you boys. Lester and I had a full life. His passing was sudden, but it was his time to go. We all have our time. You got to make every minute count."

Dexter nodded and John snored with his head cocked in the chair. He glanced at John, "Sorry about my friend. He had a late night."

She waved it off.

"You have a healthy perspective on Lester's passing. How are you holding it together? Married for almost sixty years. It must be rough."

"Oh, son. The last ten years of marriage were wonderful. Like I said, Lester was an angry man. He found the Lord, and it changed him. He loved me and served me until his last breath. I can't be mad. Whoever did this will face their own judgment. All need forgiveness. We all do bad things."

Dexter clapped his hands together and raised one in the air, "Amen, to that sister. I hope the Lord is gracious when my time comes," he said.

"Oh, he will be. Nothing is beyond the grace of God. No matter what we do on this earth."

Dexter squirmed in his seat as his church attendance in the last five years hadn't been great. He's felt the guilt of the side business and didn't know how to reconcile it with his nominal faith. The O'Kanes went to the local Baptist church growing up but more out of habit. Not because of a genuine faith.

"Can you tell me who might want to do such a horrible thing to Lester? Did he have any enemies?"

"You're sounding like those cops been coming round the last couple days. Like I told them, Lester had no enemies. He was a good man, trying to live a quiet life and serve the Lord. I think it was a mistake."

"Anybody from the past that might want revenge against Lester? When he was an angry man. Could he have hurt someone, and they wanted pay back?"

The woman released her hand from Dexter and raised an eyebrow. "Didn't you say a friend sent you over here? Why're these questions relevant? You sound more and more like the police. What's your business here?"

Dexter tried to come up with a plausible reason and stumbled over his words. "Well, ugh. My partner and I kind of help the police once in a while. We're like consultants when they need a little extra help. Our friend wants the killer stopped and so do we. We're just doing our part."

"You detectives?"

"Not exactly. We kind of fly under the radar."

"Your truck says: Antique Adventures. What's that?"

"We run an antique shop on Main. Our helping the cops is a kind of side business."

The woman nodded her head and gave Dexter a look over and didn't believe the story. "Well... I want to see Lester's killer stopped too. Don't want no other people hurt in LeClaire," the woman said with a firmness in her voice.

"That's why we're here. We love the people of this town and want justice served."

"Like I said, no one wanted to hurt Lester. But, there was that boy at church last Sunday. He was yelling at the pastor right in the middle of his sermon. You believe that? He was saying crazy stuff about people not being created equal."

"Did Lester talk to him?"

"He sure did. Told him he used to be angry. And that God changed him. God could change this angry man too."

"You think that man might've killed your husband? You know his name?"

"Anything's possible. But, he was mad. Nothing is out of question in our world today. Seen his family at church a few times. Think name's Darby."

"Anything else you want to tell us before we go?" Dexter asked.

The woman paused for a beat and pointed to a pillar holding up the porch. "Whoever did this to Lester. They left a marking."

Dexter wrapped his arms around the pole to get a better angle. The pillar had a handwritten logo of an upside down cross and a triangle as the border. A snake with large fangs was wrapped around the cross.

"What you think that symbol means?"

"Not sure. But, it's similar to our church logo. Except the cross is right side up and no snake."

Dexter took a picture with his phone. "I will see what this might mean. I assume this wasn't your doing," Dexter said, with a smile.

The woman gave him a wave off and resumed her knitting. "I think we dealing with some angry boys. Hope they find what they're looking for. Violence won't never make you happy," she said.

Dexter punched John in the arm and rose to his feet. He thanked Lester's wife and stumbled down the porch. "Hope they find the killer soon. It was very nice meeting you. We'll be in touch if anything comes up."

The woman smiled and went back to her knitting and rocking in the chair, "God forgives all people. Keep that in mind. Good luck."

Dexter and John sat in the truck for a second before leaving the house. "You couldn't stay awake for ten minutes, chubby? You missed a big clue," Dexter said, looking at his cell phone.

John rubbed his eyes and finished the last drops of Coke. "Sorry, man. I stayed up late playing the new Halo game. Almost beat it. What'd I miss?"

"Some symbol left by the killer. Man, you need a wife. Keep you on track," Dexter said, slapping John across the back.

Dexter flashed the phone at John.

"That snake looks scary."

"Apparently, Nelson's brother had words with Lester at church on Sunday. I don't know about this family. Something unsettling about the Darby's. We can't assume this kid wanted to kill Lester. I don't see a motive here, but it wouldn't be surprising with all the hate in his heart. We'll keep searching the trail and see where it might lead. Let's start with the symbol."

Dexter glanced at John.

He was already back to sleep.

30.

The think tank for Dexter and John was a converted turn of the century barn, affectionately known as The Barn. The red exterior and white trim was close to original. This was the primary location for the side business. Dexter believed the barn separated his two lives.

Dexter rolled a swivel chair up to a twenty-seven inch monitor and clicked on a mouse. John hovered over his shoulder and pointed at the screen. "That looks like the symbol on your phone."

Dexter shook his head and scrolled down the page. "Nope. Mrs. Banks said it was an upside down cross, with a triangle border, and a snake slithering around the base of the cross. That one didn't have the triangle border."

"Sorry... Mr. Perfect. I was asleep during that part, if you recall."

"I recall. You're always falling asleep on the job. Maybe less sprinkled donuts and more broccoli.

Move around more," Dexter said, elbowing John in his round belly, and dusting off donut crumbs from the desk.

"Easy, with the six keg. Keeps me warm in the long Missouri winters. Sorry I wasn't blessed with rock hard abs, like you. You don't work out."

"That's right, all natural, baby," Dexter said, flexing his gut.

"Okay, Fabio. Get back to work. Where you think we can find this symbol? I don't run with racist groups in LeClaire. Is there a local KKK hot-line?"

Dexter ignored John.

He tapped the mouse a couple times and refreshed a new website. He Googled Jarrett Stevens. "I think the racist kingpin himself, Jarrett Stevens, would be a start. If anyone is tied to the murder of Lester Banks, he'd be a person of inter-est."

The website populated and Dexter noticed the upper corner of the site. "Check out the logo at the top."

"Not a perfect match. The cross is upside down. Snake is different. You think it matters?" John asked.

"The logo on the Bank's porch was hand-drawn. Maybe it was artistic license."

"You think these racists are artistic?"

"No. But, they wanted to leave a trail. They

aren't trying to be quiet. The symbol is a statement."

"But, why kill an old man like Lester? That doesn't jive for an organization like American Renaissance. He'd be dead soon, anyway."

Dexter rose from the swivel chair and paced the room. He removed his John Deere hat and scratched his head. "If Nelson's brother was involved, maybe it was some kind of initiation. Like with gangs in big cities. They commit a crime and then are received into the gang. Maybe the killing of Lester was initiation for Danny into American Renaissance."

"Sure, but, AR flies under the radar. Stevens visits small towns and tries to recruit people to spread their message. They are racist bastards with a whacked message, yet, they aren't violent. Not a prominent national organization. Right?"

"Not sure. Don't collect Jarrett Stevens bobble heads. If they we're known for violence, they'd be smeared all over the news. Jarrett Stevens rubbed me the wrong way. He had that perfect hair and cheesy smile like he was trying to sell me something. Used car salesman vibe."

John pulled out a yellow receipt and looked it over. He held it up to Dexter, "The receipt for his order is addressed in Alabama."

"So."

"Stevens is not from LeClaire. He came to town for one of his brainwashing rallies. He bought the flag and told us we could meet him at the rally. Is he trying to set up an operation in LeClaire? Recruit evangelists for his message?"

Dexter found a chair and slumped down in it crossing his arms. "A good point. I didn't consider Stevens trying to pull something here in town. Maybe the symbol, Lester, and Darby are connected. The Darby's are drinking the Jarrett Stevens Kool-Aid."

John turned on a different computer at a desk next to Dexter. He tapped on the keyboard. "What do you think the symbol means?"

"Why does it matter?"

"Maybe there's something in the symbol that will clue us in?"

John wrote "upside down cross," in the search bar. "The apostle Peter, disciple of Jesus, was burned upside down on a cross. At least that's what church historians think. I know the Bible depicts snakes as evil or representing sin. Any connection?"

Dexter rose to his feet again and cracked his knuckles. "Maybe whoever is trying to send a message sees themselves as a martyr. Peter was a martyr for the Christian faith. AR thinks they are a chosen people. This is a symbol of persecution and misunderstanding. Yeah?"

"That would make sense. Maybe you're not all abs. A brain in that pretty face."

Dexter kicked John with his boot and sighed.

"Stop it. We need to find motive here. Who would see themselves as a martyr? That's the trail we need to follow."

31.

Dexter and John sat around a conference table in the back of Antique Adventures. Samantha served coffee as they discussed their next pick. A chime at the front door alerted Dexter to a customer.

A tall, strong, and good-looking black man leaned against the counter with a concerned look on his face. "Can I help you?" Dexter asked.

"Yeah, you can help me. You know a Nelson Darby?"

"Maybe, why?"

"I heard he might do website work for you."

"He's the best. The reason our shop is doing well this quarter. You want me to get him? He can give you a fair price on a great website. Just don't keep him too busy; we need him," Dexter said, with a smile that was not returned by the man.

"I don't know what kind of website he's been

making ya'll. But, Nelson is a racist bastard," the man said, shaking his head.

"What do you mean?"

"He took a picture of me and my girl the other day. Said he was doing a project for school. When we visited his website, it had all kinds of racist propaganda on it. Not sure why you'd want a guy like that working for you?"

Dexter paused for a second and scrunched up his face, not wanting to believe the comment. "You sure you have the right guy? Nelson Darby? The photographer who wears too big of jeans," Dexter said, as Nelson danced into the front of the shop.

"Where'd you want that new lamp on the website? I thought–" Nelson said, his face falling as he saw the familiar black man in the shop.

"How's it going picture boy? You got some nerve leading us on the other day. My girl was thinking she would be famous. When you're just a racist white boy messing with one of the few black folks in LeClaire."

Nelson backed up and a look of terror filled his blue eyes. "I didn't mean it, honest. That's not who I am anymore. It's in the past. I'm sorry," holding up his hands in surrender.

The black man shot his head up and his lip quivered. "If I had a dollar for every white kid who said what you just said, I'd be rich. You don't mean it. There's always an excuse. Upbringing, family, circumstances. Try walking in my shoes for a day. You'd think before you spoke."

"This true Nelson? You had some racist website?" Dexter asked.

"I did. Took it down. I knew it was wrong. It's who I used to be, I swear. Please don't fire me. I need this job."

The black man waved off Nelson and Dexter. "You guys work out the employment situation. I thought you needed to know. And, Nelson, I hope I never see you again," he said, slamming the glass doors on his way out.

Nelson stared at the floor and waited for his fate from Dexter.

"Not sure what to say, Nelson. Integrity is at stake for Antique Adventures. We can't have racist, or former racist, folks working here. I don't know how you grew up. I was taught to respect people, regardless of race or creed. I know it's common sense for most. But, if what that man is saying is true, I can't have you work here any longer."

"Please... don't. I like you guys. Want to keep strengthening your business. Make the website even better if you give me another chance. I'm not that guy anymore."

"That wasn't all that long ago. How could you have changed already?"

"It's not me. It never was me. I bought into all the shit my parents taught me. Questioned none of it. Now I know it's all wrong and evil. I'm changing..."

Dexter stood with his hands in his pockets and took a deep breath. "Sorry kid, you're fired. I'll send your last paycheck next week," Dexter said, disappearing in to the back room.

Nelson packed up his computer and threw a couple things in his backpack. He stormed out of the front of the store and slammed the door shut.

He stood in the front of the store, lit up a cigarette, and scanned the parking lot. A black Ford pickup sat parked to the left. Nelson squinted and noticed it was the man who had just left the store.

Nelson galloped to the back of his car, popped the trunk, and yanked out a metal baseball bat. He glided up to the side of the car and swung at the driver side window.

The man, talking on his phone, didn't notice Nelson until his face was covered in glass.

Nelson walked back to his car, tossed the bat in the trunk, and drove away.

As he zoomed by the pickup, he raised his phone and snapped a picture.

They were still very fascinating people.

32.

Dexter had called in a favor to a detective at LPD. Richard Sterns had worked for the department for thirty years. Knew every nook and cranny of LeClaire. If anyone knew about racist groups and hoodlums, it was Richard. Dexter wanted more information on the symbol at Lester Banks' house.

He ducked under a yellow police caution tape in front of a row of townhouses on Main Street. A swarm of cops, EMT's, and other people stood around and chatted.

"Found the kid dead with two contusions to the head. Looked like someone bashed in his face while he slept."

Dexter's stomach sunk and scanned the rest of the crowd. A young black woman stood with an officer wrapping his arms around her muscular body.

"Who's the victim?"

"A black kid, engaged to be married this summer, and just finished college. Whole life ahead of him," the officer said, scribbling on a note pad.

"Any eyewitnesses?"

"Girlfriend came over when he missed a breakfast date. She saw someone leaving the apartment. Didn't get an ID on the person."

Dexter walked over to the front steps of the apartment and could hear the woman wailing into the arms of the officer. "That the fiancée?"

"How'd you know?"

"I know that kind of crying. What I sounded like when my wife and kid died. Tears when the Chiefs lose on Sunday are different. Those cries are from a bad place."

Two EMT's danced a gurney down the steps of the apartment. When they arrived at the bottom, one man caught his breath. Dexter lifted the white sheet to see the victim.

"Damn."

"Hey, you're not supposed to do that," Richard said, watching the EMT grin.

"Who gives a shit? He's dead," a balding and wide EMT said.

"That's a crime scene," Richard said, looking to Dexter, "What's the matter? You saw a ghost?"

"I know the victim. He came into the shop yesterday."

Richard pulled Dexter away from the commotion and stared deep into his eyes. "You telling the truth?"

"Yeah. He came into the shop and accused our web designer of being racist. I don't forget faces. That was him, no doubt."

"You know who might've done this?" Richard asked.

"I have an idea. But, don't think it could be."

"Who?"

"My web guy. Former web guy..."

"Why would he kill this kid?"

"Maybe because he's a racist bastard? His family is drinking deep the teachings of Jarrett Stevens."

"The American Renaissance dude? What else can you tell me?"

"It's all a mess. Nelson made a website with racist propaganda. When the victim confronted Nelson, he swore he'd changed. Don't know what to believe. People don't change that easy."

Richard sighed. "That's what all racists say. They are never the problem. It's always someone else's fault," Richard said, shaking his head, and scribbling on a pad.

"He comes from a bad family. Taught him some wicked things."

"Well, your theory might prove itself right."

The detective guided Dexter to the apartment and opened the door as people rushed in and out. The room was neat and smelled of Fabreeze.

"Come in the bedroom."

Dexter paused and stared across the room to a symbol hanging above the headboard in the bedroom. It was a triangle with an upside down cross with a snake slithering around the base.

"That the symbol you sent me the other day?"

Dexter nodded.

"The one we saw at Lester Bank's house. And the one we saw on the AR website. I think we are on to something."

Richard smiled a toothy grin and his mustache grew wide. "I did a little digging on AR and the symbol. I think this will interest you. Let's meet tomorrow over breakfast."

Dexter gave him a thumbs up.

When he left the apartment building, he grazed the shoulder of the crying girl with his hands.

He mumbled under his breath, "I'm sorry."

33.

R ichard had done his homework and provided Dexter with information on the mystery symbol found at the crime scenes of the college kid and Mr. Banks.

They sat in Rudy's Diner and picked at soggy eggs and sipped cold coffee. "You ready?"

"For what?" Dexter asked.

"The symbol you found at the crime scene has dark roots."

"What are we dealing with?"

Richard shoved a manila envelope across the sticky table and nodded, "Open it."

Dexter hesitated and gave a stare. He fiddled with a couple sheets of paper and read the words. "Who are these people?"

"The triangle and upside down cross are associated with a hate-group just after the Civil War. They called themselves The Chosen. This group of white supremacists spent their days wreaking havoc on blacks and other minority groups in Missouri, Kansas, Nebraska, and parts of Texas."

"Is the group still active?"

"No. They went out of existence when the Civil Rights Movement put pressure on these kinds of groups, making segregation illegal. But, the seeds of the movement were planted, and kept alive in pockets of the states mentioned. Including Missouri."

Dexter flipped to another page and read the rest of the information. "These guys kill Lester and the college kid?"

"Don't know. But, take a look at the bottom of the article. What is the last name?"

"Stevens."

"Sound familiar? You might recall a Jarrett Stevens who visited Missouri. One of his crazy brainwashing rallies was held at the Holiday Inn Express. Well, American Renaissance is run by an ancestor with deep ties to The Chosen. Jarrett's great grandfather, Jeb, was a vital player during the heyday of The Chosen."

"So, AR is the ugly child of The Chosen? You think AR is tied to the murders? Stevens dirty?"

"Tricky part. The FBI has been following this guy for years. Despite the hateful message of AR, he seemed to be clean. Until they found this..." Richard said, handing Dexter a news clipping.

"Stevens likes slutty girls?"

"Yep. His organization is under investigation for

using monies to provide escort services for him and other employees. AR is a not for profit and is using donor money to get tail on the side."

"Where's the FBI on the case?" Dexter asked, sipping black coffee. The only way he liked it.

Richard poked at his eggs and leaned across the table using a hushed tone, "They've asked me to put together a local team to help with the case. He's still in town and they are close to taking him down."

Dexter held a finger to his mouth and promised to keep his mouth shut. "What's your next move? You find a team?"

Richard smiled, wiped egg from the corner of his mouth, and tapped the table, "Have a few guys in mind. I know you've worked a few side jobs in the last couple of years. Took down the serial killer, psycho cop, and Buffone family. Not bad for an antique dealer," Richard winked, "Good work. We need an undercover agent that Stevens and his crew would never suspect."

"What are you asking?"

Richard shrugged looking for a response.

"Two problems. One, I know Stevens."

"What do you mean?"

"I don't know him... know him. Like spending Christmas together. But, I sold him a confederate flag from the shop. Before he came into town, he wanted us to deliver a flag to him at the rally. He knows me and John."

"Perfect. He'd never suspect an antique collector would have anything to do with law enforcement. That might be a perfect cover. What was the second problem?"

"I've been hired."

"By whom?"

"Nelson Darby. He wanted me to follow his brother around. Thinks he might've killed Lester Banks. Possible connection to AR. His family sure has affections for Stevens and his message."

Richard slapped his hand on the table and scanned the restaurant, sure he had made a scene, "Perfect! These cases all work together. Sounds like you've already done homework on the Darby kid. We just need to put all the pieces together and take down Stevens."

Dexter stirred a spoon into a fresh pour of coffee. "I don't know. These racist dudes are scary. I've not done much for Nelson. I'm all for keeping LeClaire safe and seeing these scum bags taken down. But, I'm not a pure bred."

"What?"

"I'm Irish. Don't look like a stereotypical Lucky Charms variety from the homeland. But, these dudes are particular in who they protect and who they kill. My people were not treated well when they immigrated to America. My family tells horrible stories. I'm just as big of a threat as Banks and the college kid. I'm not usually this hesitant. But, something unsettles me."

Richard smiled and chewed on a piece of bacon. "No one needs to know you're Irish. You'll never get that close to them, anyway. We want you to snoop around under the radar and find more leads. Get information so we can bring these dirt bags in before they cause more harm."

"Can I have a day to think?"

"Yep. Let me know first thing tomorrow," Richard said, tossing a wad of cash on the table. "You won't be working for free. The extra cash is good for the old lady. Buy her something nice."

Dexter smiled and nodded as Richard disappeared out of the restaurant.

He stirred his coffee and thought about the racist names he was called as a child.

34.

Dexter's stomach churned thinking about talking to Samantha about the job. He had little time and needed to act fast.

He pulled into the driveway of his home, climbed the wooden steps on the porch, and glided into the kitchen. His wife, Samantha, leaned over the sink and placed a bowl on a drying rack.

Dexter snuck up behind her and covered her eyes with his hands, "Freeze. I'm looking for a beautiful blonde who's up to no good. You seen one?"

Samantha froze and smiled underneath his attempt at humor. "Not sure who you're looking for officer. There's something I need to tell you."

"What's that sugar lips?"

"This hair is not natural. I die it," Samantha said, spinning around and kissing Dexter on the lips.

"Where you been? The kid's are all in bed and your food is cold."

"I had a late meeting."

"With who?"

"An old friend."

"Well, you only have one friend, John. So who are you talking about?"

"You don't know him. He works for LPD."

"Name?"

"Richard."

"Richard Sterns?"

"How'd you know?"

"He's the one who helped you out. The serial killer and cop. Don't want to relive those nightmares."

Dexter felt his stomach do a double somersault knowing Samantha was not keen on the side business. The last couple jobs had almost cost his life and family. Swore he'd not do it anymore. But, she didn't understand that quitting these opportunities were difficult. Dexter had a calling for justice to be served.

"Yeah, those were difficult days. But, good, right? We saved LeClaire from a couple of psychos."

"True. But, I'd rather have other people worry about the evil in this town. Not you."

Dexter paused, stepped back from the sink, and placed his hands in his jean pockets. He swayed side to side and smiled at Samantha. "So, let's say there were bad things happening in LeClaire. And, maybe, just maybe, Richard asked for a favor."

"What kind of favor?"

"Oh, I don't know. One with implications for the safety and well-being of the fine people of LeClaire, Missouri. That's all..."

Samantha tossed a hand towel on the counter and placed her hands on her hips. "This is not another job. Is it?"

"Maybe. Not a scary one. Just a little undercover work to help law enforcement catch a bad guy."

"Dexter... you know how I feel about the side business. I thought you would quit. You have a family, three kids, and Antique Adventures. Why put your life and family at risk? Remember when that psycho cop almost killed me and the kids because of you dumping his sister in high school?"

"Yes... you remind me once a week."

"You're not an assassin, hit man, or whatever the hell you think this business is. You're a husband, dad, and small business owner. In that order."

"True. But, I like the side business. It keeps things interesting. Besides, it paid for this beautiful house, and the nice vacation we took last year."

"I know. But, Antique Adventures is doing well. The extra money is nice, but I want you around. Dead Dexter is useless to us," she said, batting her eyelashes.

Samantha opened the refrigerator and placed a small plate of food on the dining room table. "Here's your dinner. Meatloaf and potatoes. Your favorite."

Dexter grabbed the plate and put it in the microwave. "I know you're not fond of the side business. But, LPD could use my help. It will not be a dangerous gig, promise."

Samantha laughed, "Yeah, right. The last time you said that we almost got killed."

Dexter put the food back on the table and Samantha joined him to his right. She grabbed his hand, "Honey. I love you. And, I made vows that said until death do us part. I don't want to break the vow because I have to kill you. Or, you get killed."

Dexter jabbed his food and stared deep into the plate, afraid to look up at Samantha. With a mouth full of food, he said, "I won't do nothing stupid to hurt you or the kids. I need you to trust me on this one."

Samantha nodded. "What's the job?"

"Oh, ugh, just some surveillance work on a shady nonprofit. Trying to see if the president of the organization is breaking the law. A little snooping around and I'm out. Piece of cake."

"What's the organization?"

"Oh, you know. It's like one of those groups that try to promote racial harmony."

"Like the NAACP? Center for Equality?"

"Something like that. We think the president is running a prostitution ring and using the organizations funds to do it. No biggie."

"Sounds big. When do you have to decide?"

Dexter tried to ignore the question and took another bite. "Tomorrow."

"Tomorrow? I don't know Dex; we need more time."

"Maybe I can get an extension. But, like I said, it will be a quick job, get in and get out, and move on. It won't drag out. Half the leg work is already done."

Samantha rose from the table and stared down at Dexter. "Okay, man of the house, you sleep on it and let me know what you're thinking. Better be telling me the truth."

Samantha disappeared to the back of the house. Dexter pushed the food away as he had lost his appetite.

35.

Dexter cleared the clip on his Beretta and pressed the switch as the target screamed back to him. He examined the shots. Six bullet holes lined the center of the chest. He thought about the job and the lies he had told Samantha the night before. Dexter knew the job would not be easy. But he couldn't stop the side job.

John compared his target with Dexter's. "I don't understand guns. Can't we use other means to kill bad guys?"

John was the brains of the operation. He loved taking down bad guys with things other than guns. Like devices that looked like garage door openers that shut down the brain with electromagnetic force. At least that was how they had taken down a crime family causing trouble in LeClaire last year.

Dexter shoved a clip in the gun and gave a smirk to John. "Guns are what this country was founded on. It changed the way we fight for good. You don't want to go into a battle in hell with a water gun, do you?"

"No. But, guns are cheating. How hard is it to pull a trigger and kill a bad guy or a deer? You don't need brains for that," John said, examining his target.

Dexter picked it up and smiled. "I see why you don't like guns. That bad guy would've slept in his own bed that night."

"I'm not the best shot. But, check this out," John said, handing Dexter a pen.

Dexter held it up and watched a bikini top fall off a tan woman. "What the hell is this?"

"My newest invention. It's a killer pen."

"Isn't this the pen you bought in Hawaii last year with the extra money from the side business?"

"Yep. I got bored after playing with it a couple thousand times."

"You need a date."

John turned to the left and pressed on the top of the pen. A mist shot out the top. "See that?"

"The water coming out of the top?"

"Yeah, it's not done. That will be a mixture of mace and poison. Blind the perpetrator and kill him a few minutes later. What you think?"

"I don't know if a naked lady pen says tough guy?"

"It will when a bad guy is pleading for mercy with his eyes burning and kidneys shutting down."

Dexter fired three quick shots at the center of

the target hitting the bull's eye each time. "You can play with the pen. I'll rely on a trustier source."

"Whatever. You're just jealous."

"Jealous of what? The naked lady poison pen? Don't think so," Dexter said, hitting the center of another target.

"Jealous I'm the brains and you're the muscle. This is a thinking man's weapon."

Dexter turned to John and raised an eyebrow, "You believe what you want to believe. But, when we're pinned down by some racist psychos, I'm going into the dog fight with a gun and not a boobie-pen."

"Fine. I'll just sit over here and enjoy the view," John said, watching the top come off the woman. He smiled.

"I told Samantha about the job."

"How'd that go? I'm assuming not well."

"I kind of lied."

"Nooo. What did you say?"

"Told her it was a surveillance job. Not to worry. Done in a few days."

"That might come back to bite ya," John said, tapping the pen and giving him a grin.

"It's not a total lie, is it?"

"There will be surveillance. But, these guys will not lie down. I think we will have our hands full."

"I don't know how to explain things to her. If I say too much, she gets scared. If I say too little, she gets mad for not being honest. I can never win."

"Why I'm single."

"So you can stare at naked lady pens all day?"

"Nope. Don't need the drama. My life is full of it already. Dealing with you all day," John said, with a wink.

"I'm sure not why you're single," Dexter said, jiggling the fat hanging over John's belt.

"Carrying a little holiday weight."

"From 1989?"

John stuck out his tongue and placed the pen in his pocket. "So, you told Richard we're in?"

"Yep. I need to tell Samantha."

"Good luck with that."

Dexter didn't know how to be honest about what they were dealing with. He didn't even know what they were dealing with himself.

Dexter's phone buzzed in his pocket. It was Richard. There was another murder.

36.

Dexter paced the front of the crime scene, trying not to be noticed, and answered his
phone. "Hello?"

"You don't know what we're capable of. We are
the pure race and your kind is not welcome. You're
contaminated."

Dexter examined the phone, looking for a number. It said UKNOWN. "Excuse me. Who is this?
John, you messing with me?"

"You know who I am Dexter. We've met. Be
careful sticking your nose where it doesn't belong.
Go back to the junk collecting. It will be much
safer."

"It's not junk collecting. Its rusty gold, thank
you. I don't know who you are. But, only cowards
kill innocent people."

"These people are not innocent. They're tainted.
Born in sin. The sin of the wrong ethnicity. God

has bigger plans for the earth and it doesn't include those inbreeds."

Dexter paused and took a deep breath, trying to hold back anger. "So, what's the plan? You going to kill every black person in LeClaire?"

"If I don't get what I want."

"What would that be?"

"I'm not ready to say. The time will come. This is a courtesy call. A call warning you to stay out of this. If you want no one hurt, including that sweet family of yours, you better back down. And tell your cop friends to step back too. The nest is buzzing and King Bee is not happy."

The phone clicked dead.

Dexter wandered to the other side of the street and met Richard at the curb. "I got a call from the possible killer."

"What?"

"Yeah, a guy told me to back off. He will kill every black person in LeClaire. Something about bees."

"Bees? You sure it wasn't a prank. It's common when there are multiple murders. People looking for fifteen minutes of fame."

"Not sure. He said he knew me. Knew you, too."

"How's that possible? Did you tell anyone about the job?"

"Only John and my wife."

"How'd she take it?"

"Let's not talk about that right now. The guy on the phone sounded serious."

"I wouldn't worry about it. Let me know if he calls again."

Dexter nodded. "I don't want to be seen around the crime scene. I'm still trying to keep a low profile in the whole side business thing. I'm known as an antique dealer in LeClaire. Not a hit man," Dexter said, crossing his arms and tapping the curb with his boot.

"No problem.

"Who's the victim?"

"A young black girl. The strange part is there's no symbol. They are getting lazy or this is a random murder."

Dexter paused and grabbed his chin, "The man on the phone said he wanted to wipe out the inbreeds. I'm assuming minorities. LeClaire has diversity but not much. There is no way this was random. Not with everything else going on. Any luck tracking down Jarrett Stevens?"

"I think you're right. Sometimes groups like this will send a low man on the pole. A guy looking to move up in the ranks. Maybe he forgot to leave the symbol. Hard to know."

"Stevens?"

"Nothing. He's gone underground. But, there's rumor he's still in the nearby area. I'll keep you posted."

"What can I do? I don't want these sick bastards to do anything else. We need to keep moving."

"Well, I need to wrap up things here. I'll call you later."

Dexter went back to the car and remembered why he had the side business. The official channels of police work were always slow and often inefficient. He wanted to do something but didn't know what, yet.

The phone call had unsettled him.

37.

T he rifle lay on the bench of the pickup truck. He glanced down and took a breath knowing this needed to be done. He gripped the gun and waggled it, side to side, getting a feel for its weight. The weapon felt awkward as this was not a daily occurrence.

He peeked at the upside down cross and slithering snake tattoo on his forearm, gave it a kiss and turned his hat backwards. He unlatched the truck door and walked across the gravel road. Piles of rock shot from underneath his work boots, turning his ankle a couple times.

The gun lay across his chest like a Civil War soldier marching in a field. He turned to the right and heard voices in the distance. The man followed the trail of noise down the empty road. A dog barked across the field.

The voices grew louder and his heart beat faster as a group sitting in a circle came into view. A bonfire burned in between the group that was drinking and smoking weed.

He darted behind a tree and knelt near the roots. The gun rose to the center of the circle, with the young people giggling and dancing around the flames. He took another deep breath. Sweat poured from his temples and he scanned the sky and the woods adjacent to the field. He was about fifty yards way.

Hands trembling and heart jumping out of his chest, he tried to identify the target. He eyed one of the young people and took one last breath.

BOOM.

The bullet missed the target and grazed a metal fold up chair. A swarm of people scattered, from the bonfire, screaming in all directions. One girl fell to the dirt floor and yelled for help.

A fat kid, burned from the fire, gripped a beer and tried to save it from spilling.

The shooter took another shot and missed a second time.

The kids ran around the fire like a swarm of bees on attack. A young man eyed the target standing in front of the fire and looked for the shooter. He looked confident and unmoved by the panic surrounding him.

He pointed toward the tree where the shooter stayed pinned against the tree.

"There he is," he yelled.

The group didn't hear the man yelling and continued to run around like drunken people do.

The shooter stood and rested the gun on his shoulder and steadied his arm. He pulled the trigger, and the man crumpled to his knees.

A young woman fell down next to him and screamed. The shooter ran back down the road, hopped in the truck, and disappeared into the night.

38.

D exter adjusted his tie. Not the normal work attire of tee-shirts and jeans. He scanned the funeral lawn and looked for a familiar face.

A young man waved Dexter over as he made his way across rows of graves.

"Sorry I missed the burial," Dexter said, shaking Nelson's hand, "Wish things could be different. We cool?" Dexter asked.

Nelson loved working with Dexter but understood the firing was necessary. "Erased from the memory bank. I'm over it. Found freelance work at school. It at least pays for classes and gas," Nelson said, wiping a tear from his eye. "How's business?"

"Not bad. Hired another kid to work on the website. Photos don't pop. But, he's cheap," Dexter said, backhanding Nelson across the arm of his suit, "Sorry about Danny."

Nelson wiped his face and gave an emotionless response. "Not your problem. Hoped things would be different after prison. Danny was always hang-ing with the wrong crowds. Caught up to him," Nelson said, leaning in and whispering, "You find out anything about Danny? You know... the side business? Just curious..."

Dexter nodded. "Sorry, got sidetracked with another gig. You know if Danny was involved with white supremacist groups in LeClaire? Maybe in prison?"

"Other than American Renaissance? Wouldn't know. Why?"

"Found clues from a couple murders in town. We think the killers were connected to a white supremacist group. Might be associated with American Renaissance, or not. Hard to tell."

Nelson snapped his fingers like a light bulb went on in his mind. "The other day, I was on the side of the house getting something from the car. Heard Danny talking on the phone to Jarrett Stevens. The dude from American Renaissance."

"What did they talk about?"

"I couldn't tell. But, Danny talking to Stevens is big, right? You think they could be behind the murders? I knew Danny was brainwashed by Stevens. But, having direct access was news to me. He mentioned nothing of the sort. You think Danny could've been working for Stevens?"

"I wouldn't rule it out. Anything's possible. We're in the process of looking for Stevens. You wouldn't, by chance, know where he is?" Dexter asked, with a smile, knowing the answer.

"My family is a bunch of fan boys and racists. But, we don't have a direct line to his private mansion in Mississippi. No."

"Didn't think so. Hey, can I ask another strange question?"

"Shoot."

"You okay? For someone just having lost his brother, you seem stoic."

Nelson stumbled over words and kicked up grass on the wet lawn with his sneakers. "It's hard. I don't know what to feel. My brother was in prison for five years. I was in middle school when he left. He came back and was different. I guess I had kind of moved on," Nelson kicked an overgrown weed, "I guess, the thought of Danny killing Lester makes me sick. I don't want to be associated with that crap. Maybe I'm not letting my emotions give him the time of day."

"I get it. Sorry to question your grieving process. Everyone responds differently. I've been through this many times. And it sucks."

"Who'd you lose?"

"Wife and kid."

"I saw them the other day at the shop."

"Samantha, twins, and Lisa are a new wife and new kids. My first wife and son died in an accident. Which turned out to be a murder. Long story. Why I have the side business. Feels like my way to make sense of the universe. I owe it to them, I guess. Maybe this is part of the grieving process, who knows?"

"Shit. I feel like an ass. Sorry about your loss."

Dexter gave Nelson a high five and a smile, "No worries. You're a good kid for a recovering racist. Keep working hard and stay in touch."

Nelson gave a forced smile and found his family and disappeared across the vast cemetery lawn.

Dexter walked back to his truck and thought about Nelson and his emotions. He could've been honest about being numb toward Danny. But, his face told a different story. For now, he needed to find Stevens and end the murders in LeClaire.

39.

The neon sign showed half the letters of the Roadside Motel. Jarrett Stevens slapped the behind of a short girl wearing a tight leather skirt. She giggled and wiggled a room key and flung it open.

A smell of dirt and sex punched them in the face as they leapt to the creaky bed. They were lost in each other and didn't notice the griminess of the outdated room. Stevens slung his black suit on the floor and her clothes, which were few, were off in seconds.

Stevens didn't take long to finish.

He leaned against the headboard and gently caressed the leg of the woman, "That was fun."

The woman gave an eyebrow and held out her hand, "Not bad. Can I have my money now?"

"Wait. You leaving? Stay for a while. I have nothing until the morning."

"Sleepovers are an extra $200."

"I'll pay whatever. Money's not an issue," Stevens said, pretending to fondle a wad of cash in his hand.

"Aren't you married? Don't you need to get home to what's her name?" the prostitute asked, tapping his wedding ring.

Stevens waved her off, "It's been over for years. That's why I have you around. More excitement in a couple months than fifteen years of marriage."

The woman fluttered her eyes, "You always say the right things," she said, giving him a deep kiss.

Stevens got an erection and rolled on top of the girl. Her body swallowed by his large frame. "Why don't we go for round two? I need a do over," he said, kissing her neck.

"Oh, Jarrett, it'll cost," she said, as a bang on the door caused her to fling him to the side.

Stevens turned toward the door with his butt in the air.

"Jarrett Stevens. This is the FBI. Come out with your hands up."

Stevens rolled onto the bed and stared at the ceiling, his man parts shooting straight up, "Dammit. This is no good. Can't they give me three minutes and let me finish," he said, with a snarl.

"Why is the FBI looking for you?"

"Shut up, bitch. This is your fault. I never should've got involved with you and all your slutty friends."

"Friends?"

"You aren't the only one I'm banging."

The prostitute sat on the edge of the bed and cried, "I thought you would rescue me from this life. You lied."

"Yeah, men say things to get what they want."

Jarrett Stevens put on his clothes and opened the motel room door. A tall black FBI agent pointed a gun at the center of his face.

"Don't make things worse. Get in the car," he said, opening a car door, and guiding Stevens into the backseat.

"Please don't waste my time," Stevens said, with an evil grin.

The agent snapped back, "Not a good look for a guy with your influence to be coming out of a dingy motel room with a call girl."

"Everyone has their price," Stevens said, chewing on his fingernails.

40.

S tevens shifted in his metal chair and eyed the two men sitting across the table. He leaned back and scanned the room and smiled, "So this is where the big boys play? I figured we'd have chatted a long time ago. Not because I have anything to hide."

An overweight, balding man with a bushy mustache gave a half grin, "You think soliciting a prostitute is a sign of innocence?"

"Candy? She's not a prostitute. She's my girlfriend."

"Aren't you married?"

"A common question tonight. Men need a little on the side. I'm only human," Stevens said winking, "Hard to be a one woman man with so many fish in the sea. Right, fellas?" Stevens said, nodding at the second officer, built like a tank and who didn't find his banter amusing.

"What you do in your personal life is not our

business. But, your personal life is our business when you're breaking the law. How can you explain these?" the tank sized second officer asked, sliding a stack of photos across the table.

Stevens flipped through the photos and laughed, "Hey, he's familiar. You boys have been taking pictures of me. That' nice. Ooh... a good one..." Stevens said, locked on a photo of himself with a beautiful woman on his arm.

"You like the good-looking ladies."

"Like I said, you need a little on the side. It keeps you young."

"These ladies are prostitutes, aren't they?"

"Nah. Girlfriends," Stevens said, tapping on each photo, "Petite blonde is Candy. Here's Cindy. And, I think the redhead is Sherry. Kind of forget, so many. Having a girlfriend in Missouri isn't illegal is it?"

Both officers shook their heads, weeding through the nonsense of Stevens justifications, "For a good-looking guy, it doesn't seem like you would need prostitutes to meet your needs."

"Why do you call my girlfriends prostitutes? They are precious in God's sight. Please don't disrespect these ladies."

Tank officer stood up and pointed at Stevens, "Let's stop the games. You're running a prostitution ring. These are not your girlfriends. You might get tail on the side. But, prostitution is illegal in the state of Missouri. Fines, prison time, that's what's coming for you."

Stevens nodded and furrowed his lip, as he smiled at the small interrogation room, "I like Missouri. No Alabama but the people are friendly. I've enjoyed spreading my message here. People are receptive."

"Sounds more like spreading your seed. What message would that be? The racist nonsense American Renaissance stands for," the black officer said.

"I am honored that you like our organization. A message we are proud of. We've done great in Missouri and have found many new recruits. Things will be better in the Show Me State."

"We don't know everything about AR. But, with the prostitution ring out in the open, we have free reign to check out every detail of the organization. I don't think it would be a good look for a CEO to be caught up in side business. Donors won't be happy."

"You boys have it all figured out. But, I'd be careful. Sometimes when you think a bees nest is empty that's when it comes alive. You can search and do your little police work. You'll have a hard time finding much on me, or AR," Stevens said, leaning back in the chair and twiddling his thumbs.

"We'll see. These photos are a good start. How are you going to explain it?"

"There's nothing to explain boys. I'm getting

some on the side. These girls are not prostitutes. Got the wrong guy."

"Okay, whatever helps you sleep at night," the fat officer said, "A trial before a judge and he'll decide your fate."

"Why I have the best lawyers in the land," Stevens said, with a wink.

"You'll need them," said the black officer, as they both left the room.

41.

Dexter's phone blew up in his pocket.

"They got Stevens."

"Where is he?" Dexter asked, leaning a sign against a barn door.

"FBI took him in last night. Caught him with a prostitute."

"You were right; he was running something on the side."

"Don't know all the details, yet. But, I think American Renaissance is going down."

Dexter held up a finger to a man who was helping him load antiques into his truck. He told the man to hold on a second as he finished his call. "What now?"

"Stevens stands before a judge in the next 72 hours. They'll determine if they have a case."

"You need me anymore? If Stevens is going away, they'll connect him to the other murders, right?"

There was a pause on the other line. "A kid got killed a couple nights ago at LeClaire Lake. We think it was racially motivated."

"Was it a black kid? You think AR involved?"

"Unsure. But, some kids were having a party by the lake and a sniper came out of nowhere. Shot a kid in cold blood. No eyewitnesses."

"Identify the kid?"

"Some guy named Danny Darby. He's a local kid. They're looking into his background for clues."

"I know his brother, just went to the funeral," Dexter said, slamming the back hatch on his truck.

"Interesting. What can you tell me?"

"Nelson was acting weird. He was closed off emotionally. Losing a loved one can make people act strange. But, something rubbed me the wrong way. Now when I think about it, Nelson never mentioned how Danny had died."

"You think the brother killed Danny?"

Dexter leaned against the back of his truck and scratched his unshaven face. "Nelson doesn't seem like a killer. But, he comes from a warped family. A bunch of racists and Jarrett Stevens fans."

"LPD is looking into it."

"But, Danny was white. How would this be racially motivated? Reverse racism?"

"They've talked to one eyewitness. One kid at the lake party showed up late. He thought he saw a black man driving down the road around the time of the shooting. We'll know something soon."

"So why would someone kill Danny? Who wants to kill a guy just out of prison?"

"That's a good question. If Danny associated with Stevens, you could only imagine what shit storm he might've gotten himself into."

"You telling me I'm still needed? If so, I will need to convince my wife. She's not so keen of my side business."

"At least for a while. Let's see what comes up with Stevens."

"Keep me posted."

"Oh, one more thing. They ran the plates on the suspected truck by the lake. It came back as Lester Banks. Sound familiar?"

"He's dead. Sure they got the right vehicle?" Dexter asked.

"You get around this town. Why don't you snoop around and find out more?"

Dexter nodded and hung up the phone.

42.

Dexter arranged babysitting for their three children. He needed to convince Samantha the side business would take longer than expected. They arrived at Louie's, the best steak house in LeClaire. That wasn't saying much as there were only two decent options in the area.

A heavyset man waddled to the table and wiped his greasy hands on a white apron, "How are the O'Kanes? Haven't seen you in a while."

Dexter gave a smirk and tried to ignore the stains on the front of the apron. "Busy. Antique Adventures had a great quarter. Trying to keep our heads above water."

"I heard you were coming tonight. I'm making a special meal for ya'll. Not on the menu. That, okay?"

Dexter glanced at Samantha, who nodded and reached out a hand to him, "My husband and I honored. We need a nice meal because it might be Dexter's last," she said, raising an eyebrow.

The chef waddled away.

Dexter might've hinted on the ride over his side gig was being extended. Torn as the thrill of the fight was strong with every new case, he didn't know how to soften the blow with the case only getting its legs with Stevens on trial.

Samantha sipped on a glass of red wine, "Explain what's going on and why you still need to do this side business nonsense."

Dexter took a sip of his beer and planned the words in his mind, "Well, you see. The case is going a little longer than expected. Richard needed me for a minor piece of the pie. Now the pie is getting larger. It'll be over soon, I swear."

Samantha turned to the left and sighed and took another sip of wine, "I'm tired... tired of you putting your life on the line for strangers. When is it going to stop?"

"Honey, this is not a dangerous job. I'm just here for support. A little snooping around. Few more days and we're done."

"You didn't answer the question. When are you going to stop?"

"The side business?"

"Yes, the killing, hit man, assassin, or whatever the hell it is, business. I thought after last year's drama with the psycho cop, you were done. I think you're lying to me about this one. It doesn't sound easy. I know the look."

Samantha could read the lies on Dexter's face because they were a common occurrence for the side business. He wanted to stop. But, the jobs kept finding him. He wanted to be honest about the severity of each one but something always drew him back.

Dexter tried to downplay the lie, "Okay, the case may be a little scarier than first suspected. But, I am not putting myself or the family in harm's way. Remember, last year. That was stupid. This is nothing like that," Dexter said, feeling his stomach do a flip. He took a sip of beer.

Samantha fiddled with her napkin on her lap and glanced up with red eyes, "I'm tired, Dexter. We've been through this before. You keep choosing everything else but your family. Why can't you say no to these jobs? You have a great business at Antique Adventures. No one is making you do this."

Dexter knew that no answer would suffice. Samantha had every right to be mad because he couldn't stop. From the first job, which ironically led to meeting Samantha, he couldn't shake it. Samantha had pleaded many times for him to stop. But, Dexter had been reborn into a life of justice.

"I made a promise to some friends. They need my help. When it's over in a couple days... I'll be done for good. No more questions asked," Dexter said, knowing none of it was true. He swigged the last drop of the beer and called over the waitress. "Can you give me something stronger, like whiskey, dry?"

Samantha gave him eyes, "Careful. You have a history of not dealing with the sauce."

Dexter had fallen into the grip of alcohol and drugs after losing his family in a car accident and Antique Adventures operating in the red because of a bad marketing decision.

"Just one more. I'll be fine after eating our steaks. Can you do me a favor?"

"What's that?" Samantha asked in a snarky tone.

"Pray for me. I need divine help. I can't stop doing the side business. It's hard to explain."

Samantha ignored the comment.

They were not religious people and Dexter needed divine help.

Dexter's phone lit up with a text. It was from Richard:

The judge let Stevens go.

The steaks came to the table. Dexter smiled at Samantha, who was not interested in him at the moment. This might be his last meal after all.

43.

Dexter pulled into the parking lot of Antique Adventures, determined to make an appointment with Nelson to see if he could find more information. Specifically... did Nelson kill Danny?

Dexter leaned against the window of his truck, waiting for Nelson to arrive. He yelled at his phone, "You shitting me? He got off, like that? What good is the FBI?"

"These things happen. Judge determined that Stevens was only having fun on the side with a prostitute. Still breaks Missouri law. A few thousand bucks in fines and maybe probation. Slap on the wrist. Not enough evidence for much else."

"His lawyers must've pulled a fast one. Isn't Stevens running a prostitution ring? Got to be more dirt on him, right?"

"That's still the rumor. Our guys talked with the FBI agents who did the interrogation. Stevens acted like this wasn't his first prostitution rodeo. But, not enough for a conviction."

"How can Stevens afford to live like a king? His mansion in Mississippi, women, cars, and the way he dresses. For a guy who runs a non-profit, he's living the high life. He's gotta be making money on the side. I don't know how a racist organization like AR gets supporters in a more aware racial climate in America." Dexter said, shaking his head.

"Coming from a white man that seems obvious. You'd be surprised. The south is full of money and full of racists. I guess we'll keep digging and see what we can find. Time is running out."

Dexter slammed his fist against the window and gave a shout. "This needs to end now. Stevens is in our town. I don't want his message spreading any more. What can we do?"

"Nothing at the moment. We need to hear more on the Danny Darby case and see where it leads."

Dexter nodded and hung up the phone as Nelson trotted to the front door of Antique Adventures and peered in the window.

Dexter snuck up behind him. "Hey, kid. Long time no see. Miss having you around here."

Nelson held out a fist for a bump, "Same. I'm tiring of the freelancing gigs. I need a steadier paycheck. College and gas don't pay for themselves."

Dexter unlocked the doors and waved Nelson into the shop. "Let's grab a seat in the conference room."

Nelson tossed a backpack on the table and slumped into a black leather chair, "Be honest. Business tanking since I left?"

Dexter smiled and filled a coffeemaker with water. He dumped a scoop of coffee in a filter, "Not exactly. We've had a good month. But, our website hasn't been updated since you left. We're kind of clueless about that stuff," Dexter said, shoving the filter into the coffeemaker.

Dexter walked around the oval conference room table and settled into a chair across from Nelson. He leaned back and grinned, "So, how goes it? How's the family?"

Nelson's face turned, and he tapped on the wide table, "Okay, I guess. We're all broken up after losing Danny. I don't know if it hit everyone the same way."

Dexter nodded and put on the counselor act, "Tell me about the funeral. Why did you seem to act so weird? Like you didn't care Danny was dead. Was your relationship fractured?"

Nelson shuffled his feet and stared down, "Sort of. He wasn't part of our lives. I looked up to him when I was younger. But, he changed. When he left for prison, I kind of put him out of my mind. I wasn't sure if he'd ever come back."

"How about your folks? What do they think about Danny? Were they ashamed of his jail time?"

"Danny was their firstborn. The favorite. Despite going to jail. They didn't care. He could do no wrong. When he came back, it was like nothing ever happened."

"Is that why you were so stoic at the funeral? You didn't care Danny was gone?"

Nelson lit up, "What is this about? I thought you called me about side work? Are you not giving me the job?"

Dexter stood and glided to the coffeemaker and filled a mug, "We think Danny was mixed up in bad stuff. I want to hear your side. Any information that could help the case would be appreciated."

"What case? Danny is dead. Why do you care now?"

"I can't give details. But, Danny might be involved with a white supremacist group."

"Stevens? He talked with him on the phone. I told you that."

Dexter inched in next to Nelson and leaned over smothering him. He raised a hand to guard his face.

"What is this, man? Leave me alone. I don't need your help anymore."

Dexter whispered, "Did you kill your brother?"

"What the hell? You serious? Why in God's green earth would I kill my flesh and blood? Danny was the favorite and all, but I would never kill him, or anyone."

Dexter pushed in further, "You need to be honest. If you did, and you're not honest, things will get ugly fast. You don't want this hanging over your head, trust me."

Nelson reached for his backpack and palmed Dexter in the face, "Dude, I thought you we're a good guy. Thought you would forgive my past sins and give me a job. Now I'm getting accused of mur-der. Go back to selling your rusty crap. You're no detective. Keep your day job," Nelson said, blowing through the store and out the door.

Dexter sipped his coffee and watched with amusement as Nelson stormed out.

Confident Nelson was innocent, Dexter walked over to a computer monitor, "We still need some-one to keep up our website. And, I need to give Mrs. Banks a visit."

44.

Dexter knew Lester Banks couldn't have murdered Danny. For starters, Banks was already dead when Danny was killed. Despite a witness seeing the Banks truck at LeClaire Lake, Dexter wanted to cross Banks off the list of possible killers.

He opened his truck door and waved to Mrs. Banks, who was sitting in the same spot as before. She placed her knitting on a table and gave a wide smile, "Fancy seeing you here. How can I help you now, young man?"

Dexter removed his John Deere hat and grinned, "I needed to visit my favorite senior citizen. How are you?"

"Senior citizen... well, you're right. I can barely walk and need this contraption," Mrs. Banks said, nodding at a silver walker leaning against the porch.

"How long you been using that thing? I missed it last visit."

"Oh, a couple years. Been hard getting around the house with Lester gone. He was my strong man when I needed to get to the store or Bingo night at church. I stay home most days."

Dexter turned and stared at a full size Chevy pickup parked in the driveway. "That truck Lester's?"

"His pride and joy. Surprised he didn't leave me for it. Washed it every Sunday."

"Men and their trucks. We can't live without them. Probably because of our insecurities."

Mrs. Banks smiled. "So, how can I help you?"

"I noticed your truck had mud on the doors. Has the truck been used since Lester died? Maybe a friend or family member borrow it?"

Mrs. Banks waved a frail hand toward Dexter, "That truck hasn't moved an inch since Lester died. I never drive it. Too high for this old body," she said, nodding at the walker.

"Makes sense. The other day someone thought they saw it driving near LeClaire Lake. Any way that would be possible?"

"Nope. Unless someone stole it and took it for a joy ride. With kids these days, you never know. But, I guess not. Parked in the same spot for weeks."

Dexter nodded. He placed his hat back on his messy black hair, "All I needed today. Thank you for time, Mrs. Banks. Enjoy the rest of your day," Dexter said.

"Any closer to finding Lester's killer?"

"Inching closer every day. This will be another step forward."

Dexter drove the quiet country road and knew Mrs. Banks was right. The only way anyone could have driven the truck was if it was stolen. Dead men don't drive. And, old ladies with walkers don't drive, either.

45.

Nelson drove his Honda up Oak Grove Street where he'd lived all his life. He peeked out the window and noticed an extra car in the driveway. He parked in the street.

He opened the screen door and saw his father, mother, and another man sitting in the living room, sipping coffee.

"Howdy. Nelson is it?" a man with a southern accent asked, with a smile.

Jarrett Stevens sipped his coffee and grinned, ear to ear, scanning the small living room. "We were just chatting about an opportunity. You have a wonderful family. People ready to take my message to LeClaire. Sounds like you are a person we need on the team."

Nelson shrugged and placed his hands in his jean pockets. He was in shock over Stevens sitting in their living room. Only a few feet away in Nelson's bedroom were piles of American Renaissance magazines. Not to mention DVD's, magazines, and other propaganda pieces strewn around their racist home.

Nelson's father chimed in, "Time we take action son. When Danny died that was the last straw."

"What kind of action?" Nelson asked, not wanting to look at Stevens.

"Mr. Stevens believes the person who killed Danny was black. You know what that means?"

Nelson shook his head, "No. The police can handle it, right? What are you going to do... Kill him?"

The room shifted to silence and then an uncomfortable awkwardness like what he said was true. Mother jumped in, "We do what we have to. Those bastards will not get away with this."

Stevens raised his hands in surrender, "Not what I had in mind. But, we want to find Danny's killer. He was a vital part of my organization."

"Hold on. Danny was working for you? What do you mean he was a vital part of your organization?"

Stevens paused and looked at Rick and Nelson's mother and gave a small grin, "Danny worked for me in the joint. He scratched my back, and I scratched his. He spread my message to the incarcerated. It was a beautiful partnership."

"Yeah, even got Danny out of jail early," shouted Rick.

"Wait, come again. You got my brother out of jail because he helped you out?"

"Before Danny went to jail, he was caught in unfortunate circumstances. The altercation with the colored boy that sent him to jail was not his fault. He was my best young protégé before those scum bag lawyers got him sent to Leavenworth."

Nelson slumped into a chair and folded his hands, "Danny was not innocent. I saw the whole thing with my own eyes. You can believe what you want."

"What's that you say, son? You saw Danny hurt that colored boy? The investigators said you knew nothing," Rick said.

Nelson stared at the floor, "I was young. Scared. Didn't know what to say. Danny threatened me. I looked up to him and wanted him to think I was cool. Peer pressure, I guess."

"That's not the story I got. Danny said he was attacked by street thugs. Tried to rob him," Stevens said.

"Turn it around. Danny tried to rob that black kid. He wanted his money. It got heated and Danny almost killed him."

"Not self defense?"

"Offense," Nelson said, with a tear sliding down his face.

Rick stood from his Lazy Boy and leaned over Nelson and pressed his finger in his hair, "How dare you lie to Mr. Stevens. I know you doubt all that our family holds dear. But, to lie, and throw your dead brother under the bus like that. I am ashamed to be your father. That's not the kid we raised."

Stevens said, "I'm sorry, Mr. Darby. I'll come back. I see we are in a pickle here."

"No. You stay. This kid is the one who is not welcome. I'm sorry you had to see this," Rick said, looking back at Stevens.

Nelson slapped the hand of his father, "Go to hell, dad. You never loved me and always favored Danny. You can believe all this shit and follow this lunatic," pointing at Stevens, "I don't care. I'm happy not to believe what you do. It's what makes living in America great, right? Freedom of speech and freedom of religion. What you always taught me, huh, pops?" Nelson said, storming out the front door and into the car.

Stevens, Rick, and Nelson's mother sat in silence for a moment and sipped their coffee.

Nelson banged on the steering wheel and screamed. He dialed his phone and called Dexter.

No answer.

He left a voicemail.

46.

D exter glanced at his hand, staring at three Jacks and two Kings. He smiled at John and Gordon, who were farting between sips of beer, eating BBQ chips, and scratching their balls.

The steak dinner didn't convince Samantha that Dexter was serious about hanging up the side business. He knew deep down his family was important and he couldn't sacrifice them for his dreams of being a justice cowboy. But, the pull was strong, and he was not ready to say goodbye, just yet. Stevens was out of jail and people were being murdered in LeClaire. Enough for the risk. Even the risk of losing his family.

"Call," John said, lifting a cheek and farting.

Dexter shook his head and flapped his hand, diverting the sulfur, "Wonder why I haven't come to one of your Friday night poker games in years? I get enough of your gas at the store."

"Samantha kicked you out. That's why you're at

our awesome poker night. My gas is the least of your worries."

John was right. This cycle of getting a side gig, Samantha wanting him to stop, apologizing, and ending up on a couch, or kicked out, was common for Dexter. He was worried this might be the last straw and break the marriage camel's back.

"Sam will come around. She always does," Dexter said, with little confidence.

Gordy, a high school buddy of John's, who was almost a spitting image of his heavyweight counterpart, wiped chip crumbs off his mouth and said, "Why I don't date. Girls are nothing but trouble. I don't need that kind of drama in my life, screw em," as he tossed his cards on the green velvet table.

"You don't date because you live with your mom. And still sleep in Star Wars sheets," John said, tossing chips in the middle of the table.

"Shut it, asshole. Those sheets are worth more than your life. And, living with my mom is temporary. I'm still looking for a management position."

Dexter leapt from the table. His phone buzzed in his pocket. "I want to hear more about the management stuff in a moment. I need to take this," Dexter said, disappearing to the front room.

It was Nelson.

"Dexter, I need your help."

Dexter grinned and decided he wanted to mess with Nelson. "Who is this? I used to know a Nelson. But, he disappeared, and I never heard from him again. He didn't like what a certain someone had to say."

"Stop the games. Stevens is at my house right now. They are plotting something," Nelson said, catching his breath.

"What? Where are you?"

"I'm sitting in the driveway. I can see them laughing and sipping coffee in the living room. You need to do something."

"First, how do you know they are plotting something?"

"They told me."

"Get out of here. Stevens told you he would do something. What?"

"Find Danny's killer. And do something, not sure what. Kill him, I guess."

"You know for sure?"

"Well, Stevens wouldn't come out and say it. But, my dad was hell bent on getting this guy."

"Do they know who killed Danny?"

"They think a black guy."

"That's interesting. My friend, who is working on the case, thinks the killer was black too. Based on an eyewitness. But, I did some snooping around and I'm not sure. How would Stevens and your folks know?"

"No idea. But, they sounded serious. You gotta do something, Dex; they need to be stopped," Nelson said, pausing and giving out a whimper which turned into a sob.

"You okay, kid?"

"Got nowhere to go. Told my dad how I felt about his beliefs. He kicked me out. Can I stay with you?"

Dexter paced the front room and laughed, "Your timing is impeccable. I'm kind of homeless at the moment. Home front is a battle ground and not welcoming any civilians if you catch my drift. Wait one second," Dexter said, holding his hand over the phone.

He went into the back room and asked John if Nelson could stay over.

"You're good. I asked John. If you don't mind indescribable smells, unhealthy food, and playing video games all night, you'll have a great time," Dexter said.

"You just described the college life. Sounds like a dream," Nelson said, holding back more tears.

"It's different when you're thirty eight," Dexter said, with a grin.

"Thanks, Dexter. This means a lot. I know I didn't act great in your office. But, know I didn't kill Danny. I've hated Danny, but he was still my brother, and I don't want anyone else to get hurt."

"You bet, kid. I want justice in LeClaire, too. We need to get this Stevens character, and fast. Before anything else happens in this town."

Dexter hung up the phone and sat for a moment

on the couch. He thought about Samantha and the kids. He missed them. He wondered if he would ever see them again. Would she take him back? He didn't know but anger was boiling under the surface. There was no room for bad guys to be winning in LeClaire. He would risk it all. Whatever that meant.

Dexter went back to the poker game, covered his nose, threw down the full house and winked at Gordon and John. "Another reason you don't invite me to Friday night poker. I'm damn, good. Hope this is a sign of things to come. For God's sake, get some air freshener. This place smells like a pig farm."

47.

G ordon left the house a little after midnight as Nelson strolled up the sidewalk in front of John's house. He gave a nod as Gordon let out a fart and a smile. John stood on the porch and shook his head, witnessing the entire interaction.

"Sorry about him, kid. He's a mess. I took all his money in a poker game," John said, giving Nelson a back slap, "Come on in. The water is fine," guiding him into the living room.

Nelson tossed his backpack on a chair and scanned the room, "Never been to the John lair. Not as bad as Dexter described it," Nelson said, shaking his head and eyeing a fake Mona Lisa painting.

"What did he say?"

"Oh, not much. Just that it was a typical single dude's pad. Not spotless. Few pictures on the wall. Stacks of dishes in the sink. The Mona Lisa is nice," Nelson said, tapping the poster.

"A reprint."

Nelson raised an eyebrow, "If an original, you wouldn't live in this hole."

John crossed his arms and tapped his foot on the carpet, "Hey, easy. This is my hole. I like it."

Dexter walked into the room with a large smile on his face. He had just taken all of John's and Gordon's money in the poker game. "Nelson, buddy. Sorry I had to leave you with this loser. But, I was counting all my earnings," Dexter said, jamming a wad of cash in his jean's pocket, "Glad to have you. Never thought we'd all be back together, in John's house of all places. What's that funny smell?" Dexter asked, raising his nose in the air.

"Right? I thought the same thing. It's like body odor masked with Febreeze. More body order, and less good smelling meadows," Nelson said, with a laugh.

John ignored the comments.

"Well, we need to get down to business. There's serious stuff going down in LeClaire. We need a plan. Tell me more about the interaction with Stevens and your folks," Dexter said, waving everyone into the living room.

Nelson slumped on a flowery patterned couch with a plastic coating on the surface, "What's wrong with this couch? Is this in case you wet yourself?" Nelson asked, with John standing in the doorway.

"It was my grandmothers. A family heirloom," John said, curling his lip.

"Sorry, Dex, back to the question. I came into the house, in what seemed to be the middle of a conversation. I only grabbed bits and pieces. The gist being my dad wanted to find Danny's killer. Stevens tried to downplay the desire of murder. But, he sounded like a politician trying to downplay sex scandal. They will do something bad," Nelson said, rubbing his hands along the smooth plastic on the couch.

"You think your dad is capable of murder? Or, do you think it was just talk, after losing your brother?" Dexter asked, finding a recliner across from Nelson.

"Maybe..." Nelson hesitated, "Danny and my dad beat up a guy at a restaurant. I had an altercation at a club and he showed up at a Mexican joint. My dad and Danny beat the shit out of him in the alley. Anything is possible."

Dexter glanced to John, intrigued by the conversation, "He ever violent with you? Hit you?"

Nelson played with a bracelet on his wrist and looked around the room, "Not, really. He yells a lot. But, he never hit me, or my brother. The home was violent by proxy. AR created a violent ethos."

"Ethos? What do you mean?" Dexter asked, leaning to the front of the recliner.

"You know. The ideologies in our home weren't exactly rooted in the teachings of Jesus, Martin

Luther King, or Ghandi. More in the Hitler variety. While there was no physical abuse in the home, there was abuse of the mind. You know what I mean?"

Dexter and John nodded.

"It sounds like your dad is serious about finding Danny's killer. No problem ending a life. Especially if they were a minority," Dexter said.

Nelson nodded.

"Can you tell me something? Where are you in all of this? How you feeling? You grew up in an oppressive home. I know you struggle with the ideologies. Where are you at, in your head?" Dexter asked, in a calm tone.

"I'm confused. If you asked me a year ago, I'd be joining my dad in this shit. But, I'm changing. I see the flaws in their beliefs. Don't think it's right. No person is inferior because of their ethnicity or background. But, I had my reasons to hate the races..."

"Tell me more..."

"I had a situation when I was young. I got in a fight with a bunch of black kids. It was stupid. But, it messed with my head. It kind of fed the racist thing. I guess I never challenged my parent's beliefs because of the fight. But, I was young, and immature. I still am, but I'm seeing things clearer now," Nelson said, with confidence.

"We all change. Sometimes it takes years to realize who we are and what we want. You go through stuff to see it," Dexter said.

"I never want to go back. What am I to do? Those are my parents," Nelson said, placing his hands over his face, and trying to hide tears.

"Let's not worry about that right now. We have everything we need. I think there is every reason to believe Stevens and your father and whoever else will take matters into their own hands. Stevens needs to be stopped and is a cancer in this town," Dexter said, rising to his feet, "We all need a good night's sleep. We'll start fresh in the morning."

They all nodded.

"Before we sleep, can you spray more Febreeze? This place reeks..." Dexter said, swatting at his nose, and staring down John.

"You don't have to stay here. A nice Holiday Inn Express in town will work," John said, raising his nose and pinning his shoulders back, "I like my smelly lair..."

48.

Dexter stood at the counter of the Holiday Inn Express in LeClaire. It was a big deal for a small town, built a couple years back and not a bad place to stay. It beats the Crazy Eight Motel off Highway 152 that's full of hookers and drug dealers.

He wasn't looking for better accommodations after the stink fest at John's place. Dexter had a plan to get information on Stevens.

A petite brown-haired girl no older than twenty-five danced to the counter. She paused, smiled, and placed her hands on her hips, "Dexter O'Kane, I'll be damned. I haven't seen you 'round since that psychopath tried to hurt your family."

Dexter nodded and played the awe shucks character knowing he needed a favor, "Great memory. How's the tractor working out?"

Sandra's husband was a big John Deere collector. Dexter found a 1956 eight twenty in pristine condition on a pick. He gave it as a love offering for allowing them to stay for free at the Holiday Inn Express. She waved at Dexter with a grin, "Oh, Dexter. You'd think he'd found another wife. He rubs oil on it every night. Even caught him sleeping on it one night. Parked on the front lawn for the entire neighborhood to see. That was a very nice gesture," she said.

"It's the least I could do. You protected my family, and that is something I can never repay."

"So what brings you to the finest hotel in LeClaire?" she asked, glancing out of the corner of her eye at a computer perched on the wide counter.

"I'm looking for someone who might stay at this fine establishment," Dexter said, arms stretched across the counter.

"You know I can't give out guest information."

"Well, it's kind of for a friend," Dexter said, trying to put on the charm.

"No way, Dexter, I could get fired. Need this job," she said, shaking her head.

"One of your guests is famous. My buddy wants to see if I could snag an autograph."

"We got famous people staying here? I think the last famous person was that David someone who won American Idol," she said, snapping a piece of gum, "I sure like his music."

Dexter tried to hold back laughter as he thought the premise of American Idol was a joke. "He's not that famous. But, a big deal for some people."

"What's his name?" she asked, with puzzled eyes.

"Jarrett Stevens. Runs a well known organization in the South. He's here for some conferences," Dexter said, watching her face turn to a scowl, "Something wrong?"

"That's not the famous I was thinking of. Why would your friend want Stevens autograph? He's a racist buffoon," she said, gritting her teeth.

"I know, right? He thinks the message Stevens preaches is one Americans need to hear. I don't get it. But, he is dying of cancer and the autograph would mean a lot. Can you at least tell me his room number?"

The hotel clerk shook her head, tapped on the computer mouse, and glanced at Dexter, "My momma died of breast cancer. Horrible disease. I don't know why your friend wants a racist bastard's autograph. But, when people are dying, we give them their last wishes, right?"

She picked up the phone and whispered at Dexter, "I will do one better. Calling him to see if he can come down in person."

Dexter scrambled in his mind and wondered what to do if Stevens was in his room. He wasn't sure if he wanted to be seen at this point. He had another plan in his head, depending on if he picked up.

"Nope, not home. No answer. You want me to

leave a message for him?" she asked, covering the receiver.

"No worries. I got an idea. Why don't you tell me the room number? I'll go up and see if he's maybe wandering the halls. If not, we can try later. Sound good?"

Sandra gave a wide grin, "You know what? Great idea. I think your friend deserves to get that autograph. You go looking around and let me know what you find. Anything for you, Dexter," she said, scrolling a finger on the computer screen, "308, third floor."

Dexter tipped his John Deere trucker hat and glided to the elevators.

He hoped Stevens wasn't wandering the halls.

49.

Dexter paused in front of room 308 and thought he should knock just in case. He gave three rapid knocks and waited for a response.

Silence.

He knocked two more times for good measure.

Silence.

He leaned against the door and listened for movement.

Nothing.

Dexter took two wide steps back, leaned, and planted his work boot square on the door next to the lock. The door frame lurched forward and cracked with the force of the kick.

He repeated.

The door flung open, slammed against the interior wall and punched a hole in the drywall. Dexter walked in and touched the hole with his hand and smiled.

The racist bastard was not going to get his deposit back.

Dexter inched into the room, bathroom on the right, and bedroom straight ahead. He flipped on the bathroom light and gave a quick scan.

The counter was piled with hair products, deodorant, tooth brush, and other potions. Nothing out of the ordinary for a person staying in a three star hotel.

Dexter yanked the shower curtain back and took a peek, not sure what he was looking for. Shampoo. Conditioner. Razor. The shower was damp.

The man sure was concerned with his looks with all these products, Dexter thought.

He shut off the light in the bathroom and gently moved into the bedroom. The bed was neatly made, small black rolling luggage sat in the corner, and clothes were folded and placed in the provided drawers.

Stevens seemed like a neat and organized guy; not one that dealt with mess and inefficiency. Strange considering the potential prostitution ring and running a violent racist organization. He liked the chaos of his organization and their message but his life was nothing of the sort.

Dexter crept further into the bedroom and stood beside the end table. He inspected a stack of books on the table with a variety of sticky notes in each page.

He picked one up and read the cover: Mein Kampf. That's not surprising. Racist a-hole

Dexter pushed it aside and worked through the rest of the stack. A business book on leadership and one on running a non-profit. Nothing odd.

He reached for the last one in the stack; it appeared to be a novel. The book was a hardcover and well worn. Dexter mumbled the title: Killing Floor by Lee Child.

Dexter thought for a second and knew he'd not read this title. He was a fan of crime fiction but didn't know this one. Dexter wanted to see what the story was about but he was not sure why. He read the inside flap.

A piece of paper slipped out of the book and floated to the floor. Dexter leaned down and read the handwritten scribbles on the square paper with "To-Do" penciled across the top.

1. Order more conditioner.

2. Recruit Nelson Darby.

Dexter laughed at the conditioner on the to-do list and scratched his head over Nelson. Did Stevens already recruit him, or was this something in the future? Was Nelson lying the entire time about changing and not believing the warped views of American Renaissance?

Dexter glanced up from the paper to see a man standing in the doorway.

"I see you found my to-do list. Like to stay organized and make sure I'm staying on top of everything. You a list guy, Dexter?" Stevens asked.

"More of a seat of my pants guy. Cowboy if you like."

"I used to be a cowboy. But, I realized cowboys accomplish little. They kind of wander through life hoping something good will happen. I believe in going after what you want."

"Like going after Nelson Darby?" Dexter asked, feeling for his gun in the back of his jeans.

"Oh, Dexter, he's a sweet kid. I spent some time with his family. Good genes. Some of our greatest supporters. They're the kind of people that make American Renaissance a joy to work for."

"How do you sleep at night? Propagating a message of hate and violence? I hope God has mercy on you..."

Stevens rubbed a hand through his perfectly layered hair. It bounced as he touched it. "God and I are fine. We have similar views. There are people on earth that are wicked and must be destroyed. That's what we do. In non-violent ways, of course. Isn't that what you do, Dexter?" Stevens asked, with a grin.

"You know nothing about me. Nelson said you and the Darby's are plotting something against Danny's killer. Doesn't sound non-violent to me. I don't think you need to be playing bad cop. They don't need your help. You know anything else about the other murders in LeClaire? Lester Banks. Ray Carter."

"Here we go with assumptions. The FBI was a lot like you. Get caught with a beautiful woman and assume it's a prostitute. Unfair. Two black men murdered and you blame me. They deserved it, but, like I said, we're not a violent organization. Dexter, I'd be careful of your accusations. You are standing in my room, which you broke into. I could call the police right now. Breaking and entering. Maybe kidnapping?"

Dexter grinned, "You won't. I know too much," he said, flashing his cell phone with a photo on the screen, "This look familiar?"

Stevens smiled and leaned in for a better look on the phone, "That's our logo. Where'd you get those pictures?"

"Your logo was found at both murders. The killer left it behind. Make a statement. How do you answer that?"

"Easy. We have people all over the country that pretend to be part of the organization. Call them copycats. Not the first time, or last. Anything else I can help you with?" Stevens asked, in a calm tone.

Dexter shook his head, "You want me to believe that shit? I'd be careful. Many people are watching you. One wrong move and you're done, Stevens."

Stevens undid the cuffs on his dress shirt unbuttoned the top buttons and slipped off his shoes. "I've had a long day. Promoting the message of AR is draining work. But, I will say, the people of LeClaire have been receptive. I think even little Nelson Darby is coming around."

"Not true. He wants nothing to do with you or your racist organization. His family kicked him out for not toeing the racist line. Leave him out of this..." Dexter said, feeling around for his gun in the back of his jeans.

"I will make a deal with you, Dexter. You leave now, stay out of my business, and the business of the most important message in the world and nothing will happen to you or the people you love. I won't say anything about this little incident," he said, turning to the broken door, "And, leave Nelson alone. He's mine," Stevens said, his eyes turning to an intense stare.

Dexter brushed his gun in the back of his pants and left it alone. He raised his hands in surrender, "Okay. I'll go. Enjoy the novel," Dexter said, eyeing the Lee Child book on the way out.

Dexter headed to the lobby and saw Sandra with a wide grin, "You get the autograph?"

"Something like that," he said, leaving the hotel.

50.

Dexter ran up the steps of John's house and blew through the front door, yelling for him.

"John, where's Nelson? I need to talk with him," he said, catching his breath, and bending over at the knees.

"Calm down, boss. What's going on?" John asked, holding a bag of Cheetos.

"What are you eight?"

"I'm sorry, I've not gone grocery shopping in a while," John said, licking his orange fingers.

"You're a disgusting human. Where's Nelson? He's in trouble."

"I thought he was with you. He took his things and said he was meeting up with you at a diner."

"Shit. I was with Stevens. He told me he's trying to recruit him. Don't know what for, but I'm thinking bad things, very racist, bad things," Dexter said, still catching his breath.

John tossed the bag of Cheetos on a table and

finished licking his cheesy fingers, "I don't get it. First, good work finding Stevens. Second, Nelson said he wasn't into the racist thing. How can Stevens be recruiting him?"

"I don't know. I think Nelson was giving us a load of shit. He might be involved in whatever Stevens is doing in LeClaire. We need to find Nelson, now."

"Hold your horses, Columbo. Think about the situation. Nelson's brother was killed. Stevens shows up to the Darby's and is plotting shit. Mr. Darby kicks Nelson out for not buying into the racist stuff. How in the world would Nelson ever get involved with Stevens and his racist cronies? Makes no sense."

"Nothing makes sense right now. Stevens is dodging the FBI. Claims to have had nothing to do with the murders of Lester and Ray. Says AR is not a violent organization. He's had connections with Danny and the Darby's. Apparently, knows the killer of Danny, and wants to do something about it. Won't admit it. The trail crooked and the path unclear. Nothing makes sense. But, we're here to stop it, right?"

John licked a finger, "I don't know, Dexter. This one scares me... a lot. We might be over our heads. These KKK dirt bags make me nervous,"

Dexter took a deep breath and slumped onto the couch, "I know. Stevens threatened me when I left his hotel room. Told me to buzz off or everyone I know will die."

"Whoa, you went into his hotel room? Ballsy."

Dexter smiled, "It was one of my better ideas. I tricked the girl at the desk to give me his room number. Told her my friend had cancer and wanted an autograph. She even called his room for me."

"She didn't buy it, did she?"

"Yeah, she did. I went up to the room but Stevens was gone. So I kicked down the door and snooped around."

"Huge balls. Was the girl working the counter Sandra?"

"How'd you know?"

"Figured. She's dumb as rocks. I've run into her a couple times. I sneak into the hotel pool when it's hot."

Dexter shook his head, "Please tell me that's a joke."

"No way. You can just walk right in when a guest opens the door. Easy. I've gotten caught a couple times by Sandra. She's cool about it."

"You're something else, big guy."

A tap on the screen door startled the men as they chatted in the living room. John got up from a recliner to see who it was.

Nelson stumbled into the room. His nose covered with blood and his clothes were ripped. He looked like he had been attacked by a dog.

"I need help," Nelson said, falling to the living room floor.

51.

Dexter helped Nelson onto the couch in John's living room. Nelson's face was covered in cuts and he had dirt smeared across his forehead. He moaned and grabbed his rib area.

"What happened?" Dexter asked.

"I don't know. I went to Rudy's to get a milk-shake and clear my head. When I was leaving, somebody jumped me in the parking lot. I think it was Jarrett Stevens."

John rushed into the room with a bag of ice and tossed it to Dexter. He handed it to Nelson. Nelson placed it on the side of his face and lay back on the couch.

"You sure it was Stevens? He doesn't seem like the fighting type. More of a send a goon to do your dirty work kind of guy. His hair is too nice," Dexter said, examining the cuts on Nelson's face.

Nelson shook his head and moved the ice pack to his ribs, "I think it was him. It all happened so fast. I was leaving the restaurant and almost made it to my car. Someone came up from behind. I might've blacked out for a second. I remember little."

John stood over the couch and crossed his arms, assessing Nelson's wounds., "Where were you headed after Rudy's?"

"Home. Wanted to talk sense into my dad. See if he'd let me come back. Your place is great. But, there's a smell. Combination of mothballs and feet."

"It's my grandmother's couch. Please don't make fun of the deceased," John said, with a sullen look.

"Sorry."

"How are things on the home front?" Dexter asked.

"Don't know. My folks won't talk to me after the confrontation with Stevens. Not sure they'll ever let me come home. I hope that Stevens burns in hell. This is all his fault," Nelson said, staring off into the distance.

"Anybody else see anything at Rudy's? See Stevens?" John asked.

Nelson shook his head. "When I got my bearings, I looked around and didn't see him anymore. I opened the car and drove straight here. Didn't know where else to go," Nelson said, a tear sliding down his dirty face.

"You didn't think to go back into the restaurant

and get help? Ask if anyone saw anything? Call the police?"

Nelson shot back in a defensive tone, "What... use the pay phone? This isn't the 90's. I got the shit beat out of me. I didn't know what to do. Are you calling me a liar?"

"No... Why are you getting defensive? It seems odd, on a Friday night, no one would see a kid get beat up in a public space like Rudy's. It's a popular spot," Dexter said, smiling at John.

"Screw you, Dexter," Nelson said, sitting up, "I've had a traumatic night and you have the balls to call me a liar? Why would I lie about this? Stevens did this. He wants to get back at me. I know it..."

"Maybe. But, one thing in your story is not jiving. You said you went to get a milkshake and clear your head. I remember having breakfast with you the other day. You passed on a milkshake at Rudy's. Said you were lactose intolerant. Maybe you know something I don't know. But, a milkshake wouldn't be a good idea in your condition. Have you been miraculously healed since our breakfast?" Dexter asked with a grin.

Nelson stumbled over words, "Did I say milkshake? I meant burger. I wanted a burger. They make one of the best in LeClaire. The head trauma is making me loopy," Nelson said, holding his forehead.

John snagged the ice pack from Nelson and

tossed it on a table. Nelson looked up with shock. "What are you doing?"

"We've seen a lot of bad guys in our time. People who lie for a living. You pick up clues along the way. Like in a poker game when someone is bluffing. Your face is telling us a different story," John said.

"Go to hell fatty. I have nothing to hide. I'm telling the truth," Nelson said, shifting on the couch.

John dropped on two knees and stared into Nelson's blue eyes. He smiled, "Those cuts on your face... too clean and straight. I'm thinking razor or some other sharp object," John said, trying to touch his face, but Nelson recoiled.

Nelson leaned back. "Good one. You're telling me I cut my face to make up a story about being beat up in the parking lot at Rudy's? Why in the hell would I do such a thing?" Nelson asked.

"Don't know, yet. The cuts aren't the only flaw in your story. I noticed the pattern of dirt on your forehead."

"Come on. The dirt is fake?"

"No, the dirt is real. The problem is the streak is too straight. Not consistent with random dirt from falling in a parking lot. Or from getting in a scuffle with another person. Looks like a dirty hand wiped across a sweaty forehead. Did you fight Stevens?"

"I told you. He came up from behind me. Dirt proves nothing. So what? Maybe I wiped my head with my hands. They're dirty. Doesn't prove I wasn't attacked. You guys are crazy," Nelson said, rolling his eyes.

"Turn over your hands."

Nelson obliged.

John grabbed them and examined them with a close eye, "I've been in many fights. Usually because of the side business. One thing is off about your hands. Not scratched, cut, or showing any signs of blood. When a dude hits the deck, you can bet the hands go down for protection. It's a primal instinct. Except... you have no signs of hitting the pavement. They are dirty, yes. But, the dirt looks self-induced. Like you wiped them on the ground. Am I right, Dexter?"

Dexter peeked at Nelson's dirty hands, "Appears so, big fella. I too have been in many a fight. When you get thrown to the ground and are being punched an inch from your life, you also put up the hands to protect the face and other body parts. No signs of that. Weird..." Dexter said, winking at John.

"You guys are psychotic. This proves nothing. You're a bunch of wannabe detectives and are talking out of your ass. I don't need this. I thought you were my friends and could help. How I was wrong," Nelson said, standing up.

Dexter stepped back and John glanced up from the floor. "Weird how you're not wincing from pain any more. You came in and seemed to have a rib injury. Put the ice on the ribs, but now they are healed?"

"Stop it. I'm leaving."

Dexter grabbed him by the shoulder and pushed him back, "A more important question. Has Stevens gotten to you? Are you working with him? Did you kill those people? Tell the truth now or this gets real dark real quick."

Nelson fell silent.

There was a knock on the front door.

"LeClaire PD. Anyone home? I'm looking for a Nelson Darby," a deep voice called out.

52.

A small white and a larger black officer stood in the doorway of John's place.

"I'm Detective Jake Pope. LeClaire PD. This is my partner, Detective Richard Sterns."

John cracked open the screen door and smiled, waving the officers into the living room. Dexter waved to Sterns, and he returned the favor.

Nelson sat on the couch mumbling to himself.

"Sorry to bother you gentlemen tonight. We have an investigation that needs some follow up. We are looking for a Nelson Darby. Ran the plates on the Honda out in front. Is he here?"

John moved and Nelson waved from the couch. "I'm he," he said, with a plastic smile. "Problem officers?" Nelson asked.

The two detectives glided into the room and John offered them a seat on the couch. They denied the invitation and stood.

"We've been investigating Jarrett Stevens for a

couple months. He's been in LeClaire, for a week, doing rallies with an organization called American Renaissance. You familiar with this institution?"

Nelson snarled, "Yep. My folks are big fan boys of Stevens. He's the racist guy, right?"

"American Renaissance is not a good organization. We've been following a couple leads with suspicion that Stevens and the organization are doing illegal things in LeClaire, and elsewhere. Nothing thus far…"

Nelson furrowed his brow, "Why are you looking for me? I'm not associated with that racist bastard. He's ruined my life," Nelson said, pointing to the cut on his cheek, "He gave me these."

The detectives looked at one another and smiled, "Stevens hurt you? When?"

"Tonight. I was getting a burger at Rudy's. I think he came out of nowhere and knocked me out. These guys don't believe me," Nelson said, glaring at John and Dexter, who were standing to the side of the officers.

"You sure it was Stevens? How long ago?" Sterns asked.

"About two hours ago."

"Any eyewitnesses of the attack? Did you get a clear look at Stevens? Seems like someone would have seen something. Rudy's is busy on a Friday night," the white officer said.

Dexter and John tried to hold back laughter.

"Not sure. After I came to my senses, I drove

straight here," Nelson said, bouncing his feet up and down on the carpet.

The white officer scratched his unshaven face and glanced at Sterns. He was smiling, "Something is not adding up," Sterns said.

"Here we go again. You don't believe me either," Nelson said, huffing out air.

"In detective work, you want all the facts before you determine guilt. That's obvious. We're looking at the facts and something is off," Sterns said, reaching into his jacket and pulling out a folder. He opened the manilla folder and held up a photo. "Is this you?"

Nelson leaned toward the front of the couch to get a better angle.

He nodded.

Officer Sterns ripped out a second folder and held it to Nelson, "You recognize this guy?"

"Jarrett Stevens. His picture is all over our house."

The officer held up one last photo. "Now tell me about this one."

Nelson examined the photo. "It's me and Stevens sitting in a car."

Dexter and John peeked at one another and mouthed, "What the Hell?"

Nelson shifted on the couch and ramped up his foot tapping. "Where'd you get that? How do you know that's me? I have a common look you know..."

"The photo was taken in front of a house in LeClaire. You know whose house?"

"That famous guy from American Idol. David something..." Nelson said, looking for laughs, and getting blank stares.

"You think this is a laughing matter? The home is that of a Reggie Lewis. Name familiar?"

"Nope. Never heard it in my life."

"You will hear more about that name."

"Why?"

"He was killed tonight."

Nelson rose to his feet from the couch. "You do not understand the hell I live with. That kid deserved to die. He hurt me years ago. I don't care. I'm justified in my anger. That swamp money had to die," Nelson said, his face contorted and turning red.

"Nelson Darby you are under arrest for the murder of Reggie Lewis."

Nelson shook his head, glanced at the floor, and then back at the officers. He smiled, slapped the folder out of Sterns hand, ducked under the reaching arms of Sterns, and bolted for the door, almost ripping the screen from the hinges.

The guys and the officers were stunned by Nelson's quick maneuver. Officer Pope pulled his gun and Sterns scolded him to put it back.

Nelson ran into the street when a black sedan swung open the door and he jumped in. The car sped off, squealing tires and red lights disappearing into the night.

The men stood at the door.

Officer Sterns called in back up.

Dexter said, "You can't trust a racist."

53.

S tevens spoke in hushed and calm tones, "How'd it go?"

Nelson caught his breath and turned to check the back window for anyone following, "The cops showed up. Those idiotic antique collectors figured out the fake story. I knew this was a bad idea," Nelson said with panic.

"It'll be fine. The cops in this town are morons. They haven't been able to stop me yet. And I'm counting on them continuing their record of incompetence. We'll be on a jet to Mississippi in a few hours. Problem solved," Stevens said, with a grin, staring at the empty road.

"Just like that? You are banking on the morons that are LPD to not find us. They accused me of murder. I can't go to Mississippi."

"Mississippi is home base for American Renaissance. We will continue to spread our message near and far. We did well in Missouri, if you ask me,"

Stevens said, sliding a hand slowly through his gelled hair.

Nelson grabbed his head, "What the hell have I done? I killed Reggie. Dexter and John know too much. I'm going to prison forever. You did this... I didn't want this. You said everything would be fine. It's not fine," Nelson said, leaning against the window, and staring out into the streets of LeClaire.

"Didn't it feel good?"

"Did what feel good?"

"When you pulled the trigger. Watched that monkey bleed out on the floor. You said that's all you wanted in life. Revenge."

"I thought it was what I wanted. I don't feel better. That kid didn't deserve to die. He hurt me a long time ago. It was a stupid basketball game. Dammit. My parents brainwashed me with all this hate. You brought that damn message into our home. Danny is dead. Reggie is dead. Those other men are dead. And I will be dead, in the electric chair."

"You don't get it. You are nothing like your brother. You're weak and don't embrace the core tenets of our faith. This is not what I trained you for."

"Shut up. You lied. You only cared about me because Danny died. He was the one to take over the organization. When he died, you looked for an easy target. I should never have taken the money."

"You little shit. You had no problem taking my money. A little heat in the kitchen and you change your mind. You had no trouble killing Danny. Making that scene at your house and fooling your parents. What good are you now? I should drop you off here and let the moronic LPD find you."

Nelson didn't respond.

"You owe me. We still have one more job before I leave for Mississippi. It is the reason I came. You in? If not, I leave you on the side of the road, and you fend for yourself. Those cops will be coming any minute," Stevens said, staring intensely at Nelson.

"Fine, last one" Nelson said, still staring out the window.

54.

"**D**ispatch, we are in pursuit of a possible J-10. Please send all available back up," Sterns said, attaching the radio to the dashboard.

He slapped Jake Pope on the leg and shook his head, "Come on young buck. You let that kid run right out the front door."

"I didn't see you make much of an effort, old man," he said, scanning the road straight ahead.

"Too old for that stuff. I'm getting a pension soon and need not tear an ACL before I visit Europe."

"Europe? You don't seem like a Europe kind of guy."

"Why? Because I'm black?"

Pope stumbled over his words, "No... I just meant, ugh..."

"What black folks can't have nice vacations? Experience culture?" Sterns said, giving him a glare, while gripping the steering wheel of the undercover police cruiser.

"I will shut up now. Focus on the job."

Sterns nodded.

The radio squelched back. "This is dispatch. Please advise."

"This is Detective Sterns. We are in pursuit of two white males, driving a black sedan. Nelson Darby is a possible murder suspect. We believe they are armed and dangerous."

"We have back up in the area," the dispatcher said.

"Don't know where they're headed. I will update in a moment."

Jake pointed straight ahead to a black sedan that veered to the right, down a side street. Sterns ripped the wheel to the right and pressed on the gas, to get close up to the speeding car.

"Get ready, kid. This could get ugly in a hurry. We don't know what these two have in mind. The racist and the murdering kid is not a duo I want to mess with. Don't need this right before retirement. That's for damn sure..."

Pope watched the sedan swerve down a country road, "That way," he said.

Sterns pressed further down on the gas, as the Impala revved with power, gaining on the other car.

A plume of dust shot up in front of the vehicle and the tires rumbled on the gravel road.

"Where the hell they going?" Pope asked, shifting in the front seat, trying to see through the dust cloud.

Sterns said, "Keep an eye on them. Don't want to lose those bastards."

Sterns slowed the car down as his vision was getting worse with each mile. "I can't see shit. Need to get out of their dust."

"No, drive, old man. They are right in front of us," Pope said.

"Excuse me. You're not the one driving the car. I can't see a foot in front of my face. Not about to drive into a ditch and jack myself up before Europe."

"Shut up about Europe. Just drive... Faster..."

Pope scanned to the left and the right of the cruiser, "The dust is settling. I think they turned. Where the hell are they? I don't see them anymore."

Sterns checked the driver window and then looked back at the rearview mirror. "Shit. They're gone."

He pulled the car to a stop, shifted to park, and unlatched his pistol from the side of his black pants. "I'm getting out for a better look," he said, glancing to Pope.

Pope unlatched his gun and slowly opened the car door.

The dust from the gravel road dissipated and Sterns caught a view across the road. An old house was perched a few hundred yards away. The black sedan was parked in the driveway.

No lights were on in the house and it appeared to be abandoned.

Sterns glided across the road and waved Pope to follow. They scanned the yard and noticed a creek that ran around the perimeter of the broken down house.

"Back me up, young buck. We're going to the house."

Pope drew his gun and waved it around the yard and followed on the heels of Sterns.

55.

Dexter fired up the Ford F-150 and glanced over at John in the passenger seat. He was smiling and playing with a pen, "Please tell me that isn't the naked lady pen." Dexter said, opening the glove box, and tossing a Beretta on the bench seat.

John laughed, "I love this pen."

"You figure out the poison part? Not sure how useful it will be. But, does it work?"

John stuck out a tongue, "Like a charm. I told you I'd get it working."

"Whatever. You play with your naked lady poison pen and I'll worry about catching the bad guys," Dexter said, turning to look out of the back window, and peeling out of the driveway.

John jammed the pen in his baggy sweats. "Sorry, boss. I'll put it away. I'm in. Let's go... You know where to find these guys?"

Dexter smiled, "Can you believe how Nelson just ran right out the front door? Ballsy move for someone accused of murder. I couldn't believe Pope and Sterns stood like statues. Those morons. I guess that's why LeClaire needs people like us," Dexter said, slapping John a high five.

"Easy, Dex. Sterns is no moron. He's a good detective. But, it was fun to watch," John said, sipping on a plastic cup of Cherry Coke.

"You had time for a Coke? Glad you're taking this seriously," Dexter said, shaking his head.

"Need fuel for the fight. How are we going to find these guys?"

Dexter raised a finger to hush John as he held a cell phone to his ear. He called Sterns and waited for an answer.

Nothing.

"Sterns is not answering. I'm hoping he can tell us where they are. We can lay back and see if they need our help if things get ugly."

"Feels weird not being the ones to get the bad guys. Those detectives are out in front doing our job."

"Sterns is a good cop, but he's old. Never hurts to have backup. I think the job ended when Nelson turned out to be a liar."

John nodded and took a sip on the Coke.

"Never trusted that guy. Always felt he was only telling half truths."

"I get it."

"What?"

"How many times did you tell me to fire the kid?

But, I should have let go of this mess a long time ago. My wife hasn't talked to me in days."

"How's your head?"

Dexter hesitated. A hesitation he was not expecting. "I don't know. It should bother me more than it does. Maybe I'm not the family guy I thought I was. Maybe this is the life I'm created for," he said, staring out into the night.

"This life? I'm fine with chasing bad guys once in a while. But, like, all the time? That's a little too dangerous for me."

"That's why I'm the cowboy and you're the... not sure what you are. I'm the brawn and you are the brains. That works,"

John raised a flabby arm and gave a weak flex of his bicep, "That's fair. But, you and Samantha, and the kids, are a great family. When this blows over, everything will work out. It always does..."

Dexter ignored the comment.

Dexter tried the cell again. Sterns answered, "We are off Country Road Lane. Head left down the gravel drive for a couple miles. You will see our cruiser and an abandoned house. No hurry. We'll have this wrapped up before you get here. Be safe," Sterns said, stepping out across the gravel road toward the abandoned house.

"Found them. Lock and load. We're ready to play," Dexter said.

56.

P ope slithered in behind Sterns and almost tripped on the back of his shoes. "Give me some space kid. Cover my right side and I will check the left. I don't see them, yet," Sterns said, his gun drawn and aimed at a window on the left side of the house.

A broken window revealed a shadow moving in the house. "I see something," Sterns said, peeking to Pope, who was aiming his gun at the right side of the house.

A bird flew out of the broken window and Sterns grabbed his heart, almost dropping his gun, "Damn bird gave me a heart attack. "

Pope smiled. "Real tough cop," he said, with a wink.

Sterns stood from a crouched position and scanned the right and left side of the property. The creek echoed in the background. "What the hell?

Their car is here and they are nowhere to be found. I think we need to check the back of the house."

Pope nodded.

His face turned to a sour look, like he wasn't sure how to complete a math problem. He grabbed his chest and pulled away his hand. It was covered in blood.

Pope dropped to his knees and slumped to the ground. Sterns ran over and lay over the body, leaning back to aim the pistol in the air.

He dialed a cell phone, "This is Detective Richard Sterns. My partner is down. I need back up. 782 West Country Road Lane. Now!" he said, in a frantic tone.

Sterns body pumped with adrenaline. He leaned over Pope, who was not making any noise.

Damn. Where the hell are those bastards?

There wasn't any sound of a gun.

Where are they? Hold on young buck. Help is on the way.

A shadowy figure emerged from the left side of the old house. He walked with no real hurry and smiled as if Pope wasn't lying on the ground in a pool of blood.

The moonlight shown on the figure whose hair was in perfect shape. Not a follicle out of place.

He raised his hands in surrender, "I see your friend is in bad shape. That wasn't supposed to happen. My partner in crime is a lousy shot. That bullet was meant for you," Jarrett Stevens said, brushing a hand through his hair.

Sterns aimed his gun between his eyes and grinned, "Strange you'd come to battle without a weapon. You're not that stupid... Stevens. I've been following you. You're a smart guy. Hard to nail down. But, this might be both of our lucky days. This will end tonight and the people of LeClaire can rest easy."

Stevens smiled and acted with a calmness not matching the stress of the situation. "I've enjoyed my time in LeClaire. Many sweet people here. Even recruited a few locals for spreading the most important message in the universe," Stevens said, fixing a hair that was out of place.

"Unfortunate. I'm guessing most of them don't know the first thing about American Renaissance. And the shady organization you run."

"Haven't we been down this road, detective? I sat before the judge. Nothing to pin on me. Why don't you stop the accusations before it gets you in trouble?"

"Your so-called girlfriend turned out to be a prostitute. That's something. Guessing a smooth talking lawyer persuaded the judge to look the other way. Or, you could be a lying racist asshole who will burn in hell. Soon, very soon. One thing for sure, we have something on you now..." Sterns said, inching closer to Stevens, the pistol rising slightly with each breath.

Stevens fondled his hair, "What have you found, detective? I'd love to hear."

"Accomplice to a murder is serious. You and Nelson Darby caught in the act. Remember, we've been following you. I'm sure when we dig around, we'll find more dirt. Like the murders of Lester Banks and Ray Waters. Oh yeah, and the state of Missouri is a death penalty state."

Stevens gave a half-smile and kicked a pile of dirt with his brown Italian boots, "I'm sure those men deserved to die."

"Why is that?" Sterns asked.

"They're not the superior race. They were born into the wrong lineage and were taking up space in God's precious world. You know the AR message. Isn't that right Detective Sterns?" Stevens asked, in a calm tone.

Sterns bit his lip and tried not to pull the trigger.

"Where's your little accomplice?"

Stevens rubbed his hands together and smiled. "Let's not worry about Nelson. He's a coward and I won't need him much longer. I'm here to chat with you, Detective Sterns.

"Want to take a walk down memory lane? We have a history that goes back much further than the last couple of weeks..."

Sterns raised an eyebrow, aiming the pistol at the center of Stevens' chest.

"This ought to be good."

57.

Sterns wobbled the gun as sweat poured from his balding head. He glanced down to see if Pope was breathing. He wasn't.

"I don't know what you're talking about Stevens. Before taking on this case, I'd never heard of you before. You're delusional. No walks down memory lane for me."

Stevens turned to face the rundown house and pointed at the door, "That house looks familiar?"

Sterns angled his head, as Stevens was blocking his view, "Looks like every old farmhouse in LeClaire."

"Come on, Sterns. Remember what took place here? The reason I'm standing in front of you."

Sterns shook his head side to side.

"Ok... I'll tell you. This is where my people killed your father. Strung him up right there on the porch."

"That's a lie."

"No, sir. We were only kids back then. But, if I recall. I think you were crying over by that tree," Sterns said, nodded to an oak on the right side of the property.

Something clicked from the past. A memory, from a locked region of the brain, opened.

"The Chosen," Sterns mumbled under his breath.

"Did you say something? Sounded like you said The Chosen?"

"The white supremacist group who killed my father," Sterns said, his gun wobbling, and a tear forming in his eye.

"It's how I got my start. I saw what happened and thought: That's a message worth sharing with the world. A cause worthy of dying for," Stevens said, rubbing his thin hands together.

"Why were you there? You're not from Missouri."

"The Chosen was a traveling band. Kind of like the organization I run. They were in the area and spreading their message and I got to go along. Life changing... I've waited for this day most of my life."

"Why do you care? I did nothing. I was just a kid. You killed my father. Isn't that enough?" Sterns asked, tears now streaming down his face.

"Shut up. Oh, shut the hell up," Stevens said, moving in closer, pointing toward Sterns chest, "You know what you did. Don't play dumb. It may not be on your record. But, you know..."

Sterns stepped back, gun wobbling, and smiled, "I'd do it again."

"Sounds like an admission of guilt," Stevens said, moving in closer to Sterns.

"Your father deserved to die. He destroyed my family and other communities with his racist agenda. I needed to stop it. The Chosen are the spawn of the devil's work."

"You call it evil; I call it the Lord's work. When you try to persecute the faith, it only grows stronger. American Renaissance exists because of you. Call it a spin-off of The Chosen. A new and improved version, with even more power," Stevens said with a wide grin.

Sterns gave a forced smile, "The difference tonight is I have the Law on my side. I have every reason to shoot you dead right here and right now for killing my partner. We'll call it self-defense."

"Nice fairy tale. I've played this story in my head for many years. You tried to stop the movement once. But, you'll not succeed twice. One less monkey on the earth will get us closer to a pure America. This is a Happy Ever After ending."

Crack.

A shot rang out from high in the trees.

Sterns gun fell limply from his hand. He mouthed, "Why?"

He fell to his knees and stood steady for a moment. He glared at Stevens one last time before he slumped down into the grass.

Nelson came running out of the darkness and smiled, waving a rifle. "Did I get him?" he asked, standing over the body of Sterns.

Stevens nodded, kicked the body, and grinned as he gloated over Sterns, lying in a heap on the ground. "This is why I came to LeClaire. Well done, son. I underestimated your ability. Two guys in one night. One is white, but who cares, death by association. Already contaminated from working with this monkey. You're no Danny, but good work," he said, kicking Stevens again.

A voice came from across the yard. The dark figure emerged from the shadows. "Step away from the body. You aren't worthy to be near a man like Richard Sterns. Served this community in ways you'll never understand. You sick pig," Dexter said, aiming his Beretta, first at Stevens, and back at Nelson.

Nelson tried to raise his rifle.

"Nope. Don't do it. I'll shoot your arms off. You'll never take another photo the rest of your sad life," Dexter said.

"Dexter O'Kane. Fancy seeing you here. But, like these incompetent detectives, you're late to the party. It looks like they are enjoying heaven, or burning in hell. I'll guess the latter," Stevens said, raising his hands in surrender.

"Hell... for all you've done. I think a special room of torture has been reserved for you. Special cases like you. If you play it safe, you don't have to find out tonight."

"Oh, Dexter, my silly Irish friend, you can go back to your little junk collecting business. I already got what I came for."

"What's that... like... four murders now? Is that why you came?"

"I came for this one in particular. Richard Sterns is not all he's cracked up to be. He's done bad things."

"Let's not compare apples to oranges. Sterns has done nothing wrong."

"You consider killing my Father right or wrong?"

"That's bullshit. He doesn't even know you."

Dexter lowered his gaze and could see the honesty in Stevens' eyes.

Nelson lifted his gun and tried to get off a shot. A man from the left lunged into Nelson, knocking him to the ground.

John lay over top of him, pressing an object into his neck.

The naked lady pen.

58.

J ohn released the pen from Nelson's neck. He coughed and rolled around on the ground. A stream of blood raced down his neck.

"The poison will hit your system in a few seconds. You won't feel a thing. We believe in humane ways of killing bad guys," John said, glancing at Dexter, and giving a wink. "Told you I'd get it to work."

Stevens watched the entire scene and didn't seem concerned or moved by any of it. "Let him die. He's no good to me anymore. I got what I needed."

Dexter held his pistol on Stevens and sauntered over to Nelson. "Sorry it had to end like this, kid. We thought you were one of the good guys. Didn't drink the AR Kool Aid. I guess we were wrong.

Nelson's eyes rolled in the back of his head as the whites fluttered. He coughed a couple times. His head cocked to the side, and he stopped breathing.

John yanked a gun from the back of his pants and aimed it at Stevens. "You're not getting out of this tonight."

"Oh, fat man. I'd be careful what you say. The night is still young. What makes you think I don't leave here unscathed? LPD and the FBI showed their incompetence already. Two junk dealers any different?"

"These two junk collectors aren't scared to get their hands dirty. With two guns pointed at your head, I like our chances."

"You wouldn't shoot an innocent man? Nelson is the killer. I was kidnapped and brought to this place."

"Who will believe that story?" Dexter asked.

"Well, boys, you're not here on official police business. What will you say when the cops arrive? I assume they are in route," Stevens said, fiddling his thumbs, looking bored.

"Don't worry about us. There's a lot of sympathy for citizens taking the law into their own hands when it includes a racist murderer. We'll be fine. What's your move Stevens?"

"My time here in LeClaire has come to a close. I got what I came for. Mission accomplished. I thought it might get dicey, so I called for backup."

A Cessna 172 banked to the right and back around over the abandoned house. The men stared up into the starry night sky.

It landed in a field behind the house.

"It's not my jet. But, I was running out of options. Here's the deal. I will get on that plane and never see you again. If you try anything funny, you'll all be meeting me in hell."

Two wide shouldered men, looking like they just ate someone, came from around the house with guns drawn. One aimed at Dexter and the other John.

"What do you think? You're just going to hop on a plane and everything will be forgotten? There are a lot of bodies in this town with your name on them. And who knows what other shady stuff you're doing with AR?"

Stevens laughed and turned to the men who were now standing behind him. "I'm innocent. You have nothing on me. I'll go back to my homeland of Mississippi and enjoy the next chapter in spreading the most important message in the entire world."

"Just like that... you think no one will come looking for you...?" Dexter asked.

A groan came from behind the men.

Sterns rolled to the side, gripped his pistol with two hands, and fired a shot in the center of Stevens' face. Brain matter and blood launched in all directions.

"Sorry... your message ends tonight."

The two body guards tried to get off a shot before John and Dexter laid them down with two quick shots.

Sterns slumped over, moaned and wheezed in a growing pool of blood from his right arm. Dexter leaned in on him and assessed the wound. "You will make it," he said, pressing on the blood soaked jacket of Sterns.

"Hope so. Going to Europe in a couple months," Sterns said, with a crooked smile.

He blacked out.

The LPD raced onto the scene, followed by ambulances and fire trucks.

Dexter and John jammed their guns in their pants and held up their hands.

We want to file a citizen's arrest.

59.

J ohn and Dexter sat in front of Antique
Adventures and enjoyed the warmth of the
summer day. Dexter had an Iced Tea and John a
Diet Cherry Coke. They rocked back and forth on
two wooden rocking chairs.

"I went to Mrs. Banks' house," Dexter said, taking a sip of his tea.

John furrowed his brow, "Remind me again?"

"Lester Banks' wife. The one killed by Stevens'
crew."

"Got it. What did you say?" John asked, sipping
the Coke.

"Nothing much. Just wanted her to know justice
had been served. Stevens won't hurt anyone in this
town any longer. And, it turns out Nelson stole
Lester's truck to kill Danny. It wasn't a black guy
who killed him."

"What did she say?"

"You know, she was thankful. She talked about

forgiving people. I don't know how you're supposed to do that with a guy like Stevens. Or Nelson. They're beyond grace, right?"

"I'm not one to judge. I need all the grace I can get. I'm no racist murderer, but, I got my own issues."

"True. We all do. You think I can change?"

"What do you mean? If you're referring to the verbal assaults on the Vice President of the company, there is no hope for you," John said, with a wide smile.

"Harassing you would be like breathing. What I mean is... the side business. You think my desires can change? That damn job keeps ruining everything around me. But, I can't stop."

"You've got to make choices, man. Samantha's not talking to you right now. Consider hanging up the pistol for a while."

Dexter became animated, "John... you have to admit seeing Stevens and Nelson die and justice being served is like the Coke I used during my season of depression. It's damn hard to quit. Shit... what am I thinking? I can't choose work over family. Can I?"

"You might've answered your own question."

Dexter and John sat in silence and enjoyed more Iced Tea, Cokes, and sun.

A heavy set man with a beard strolled up to the front door of the store and removed his straw cowboy hat. "Sorry to bother you boys."

Dexter flinched when he realized who it was. "You're the former KKK guy. We picked at your place," Dexter said, raising his hands in surrender.

"Put your hands down. I won't hurt you. I came to apologize."

"Huh?" John asked.

"I wasn't fair to you when you came by my place. That KKK stuff was a past life. A life I ain't proud of. Please forgive me. I shouldn't have threatened you."

John and Dexter nodded.

Dexter said, "If I'm not mistaken, I might have said some things too. Sorry..."

The KKK guy brushed it off.

"Kind of strange question. You related to Nelson Darby?" Dexter asked.

The man nodded. "Yes, sir. You hear he was killed the other night. He was involved with that Stevens character from American Renaissance. That's too bad. He was a good kid. A photographer. We had Thanksgivings together with our families. His dad is my brother."

John slapped Dexter on the arm and mouthed, "told you."

"That explains a lot."

"What?"

"Nothing. Thanks for stopping by. Sorry for your loss. Come back any time and check out the rusty gold. Got some Confederate flags inside... sorry, bad joke," Dexter said, turning red.

The large man ignored the joke.

He tipped his hat and put it back on his sweaty head. "If you boys want to come by and see my collection, please do..." he said.

"We'll think about it."

The man disappeared down the street in his Chevy truck.

John clapped his hands together. "I knew they were related. We should have fired that kid a long time ago. You need to listen to me more. Not just a pretty face... not just a pretty face..." John said, sipping his Coke.

"Okay, okay. But, that's an irrelevant point considering the circumstances."

"Who knows? Maybe none of this would've happened. If you listened, your life would be a lot more fulfilling. That's for sure."

"I'll take note. Did I tell you Sterns and Pope made it through surgery? Pope will be back to work next month."

John smiled, "That's great! Did Sterns retire and make it to Europe?"

"Yep. But he had to wear a sling for the entire trip. Not a bad tradeoff for killing the guy who was part of the group who murdered his father. Crazy, right?"

"You want to talk about forgiveness. I don't know how you can go on after seeing that. Maybe there is justifiable murder?"

"I don't know. But, let's make sure wherever this

side business leads, we are doing it for the right reasons."

"Deal. I need to figure out what those reasons are."

Dexter finished the last sip of Iced Tea and walked inside the store. He flipped over the Open sign.

"Damn. You know what I just remembered? We need to find a website guy. Our site sucks balls. Maybe you can do it?" Dexter said, slapping John on the back.

"If you just would have listened, things would have gone better for everyone. And no way in hell I'm doing the website. I'm too busy... new Zombies 4 game coming out soon."

Dexter sighed.

Antique Adventures was open for business. LeClaire was safe for at least another day.

60.

Epilogue

Dexter reached into the mailbox attached to a pillar on his wide front porch. He sifted through the bills and noticed two small envelopes.

He opened the first, addressed from Rome, Italy. Dexter smiled knowing who it was from, "Hope this postcard finds you well. We made it to Europe, and it was amazing. I didn't have time to tell you how much your friendship means. Official police work is done and there will be great memories to relish. You are not a bad cop, Dexter. I know you don't work in the official capacity, but thanks for keeping LeClaire safe. And, please tell no one, about, you know, the family drama. It will be our secret. Your friend, Richard Sterns."

Dexter grabbed a rocking chair, on the porch, and slumped down. He shuffled through the rest of the mail and laughed about the letter from Sterns.

It was something he could laugh about now considering the dark situation they had taken care of.

He opened the second letter which didn't have an address on it. He squinted at the small print, "Dexter, this letter was long overdue. I know we have tried to make things work. We met in stressful conditions and did the best we could with our different lives and families. I thought this was the life I wanted to live. I didn't think living with a cowboy would be a problem. I told myself that I'd adjust. But, the last couple of years have been hard. I don't feel safe and don't think the kids are either. That's all that matters. It seems you've chosen other priorities," Dexter paused, holding the letter to the side and shaking his head, "And that's hard to take. Hard to understand. I will make it easy for everyone. I know you want things that don't involve family. Well, I am leaving LeClaire And I'm taking the kids. We can work out the details later. I'm not sure if I'll ever see you again. When you get this letter, our stuff will be gone. Good luck, Samantha Rose."

Dexter slammed the letter on the porch, ran into the house, and saw the kid's room was torn apart. He ran to his bedroom and Samantha's part of the closet was empty.

Dammit. Samantha meant business. She did it. She's gone.

Dexter went back to the porch and sat in the rocking chair to think.

He knew, deep down, Samantha was never coming back. But, it was real now. Maybe the life he wanted didn't include being tied down to family. An idea he had never thought possible. Not to see his kids and Samantha's beautiful face would be a void. But, maybe it was not a big enough void to drop the side hustle.

Maybe it was a void that needed to be filled with something else? The else was not clear at this point.

Dexter waited for tears. Nothing.

Dexter's phone buzzed in his pocket. "This is Dexter."

The man on the line sounded chipper, "Hey, this is Pope; Richard Sterns' former partner in LeClaire. Well, sorry to bother you. Need to ask a favor."

Dexter smiled, "This better not be a surprise party for Richard. He hates those things."

"It's about a job."

"I have plenty of work at the moment. But, what kind of job? Please tell me there are no more racist psychos in LeClaire," Dexter said, chuckling under his breath.

"Not that I'm aware of. I'm back in LA. The job is here. There are plenty of psychos here if you're interested. Interested?"

Dexter hesitated and couldn't believe all of this was happening in such short order, "Like a detective job? I need to think about it. Things are a mess right now. Family stuff. Can we chat later?"

"Yeah, like a detective job. But, how you like it. Undercover and off the record. I need to know soon."

Dexter tapped on the arm rest of the rocker, "How much time I got? Kind of burned out."

"Need an answer soon. Psychos are on a different timetable than us. I think you'd be perfect."

Dexter grinned at the flattering statement, "I have your number. I'll get back to you."

He hung up.

The phone rang again. It was Pope.

Dexter ignored the call.

He rocked in the chair and lit up a cigar.

Can I get a break for a minute? I guess crime never sleeps.

Dexter would be lying if the job in LA didn't sound interesting. He guessed, when crime fighting got in the blood, it was hard to get out.

Authors Note

Race is not a topic discussed enough in America. We live under the assumption racism vanished with the abolition of slavery post Civil War and disappeared with the heroic efforts of Martin Luther King in the Civil Rights Movement. But, depending where you live in the country, it's alive and well. Albeit we have made tremendous strides in the fight for racial injustice, we still have a long way to go.

Color Blind was cathartic in an odd way. I am a white man living a privileged middle class existence and naïve to the realities of racism. When I decided to place Dexter, John, the Darby's, and Jarrett Stevens in LeClaire and center it around racism, I wasn't sure how it would turn out.

When I began the project, I lived in a predominantly white neighborhood. By the time I finished, we were living in the inner city where my family is the minority.

Maybe the story was for me, a way to deal with

my own bias, and prejudice? Some say fiction can heal the soul. I think there was some healing going on for me, and maybe you.

But, like all the Antique Assassin books, I use humor. We are stupid humans most days and don't know which way is up. It is good to laugh at ourselves and the mess we have made. While the subject matter is serious, I hope it was still a fun read, and allowed you to escape for a couple of hours, forgetting about the struggles of life for a time.

In my own voice, and unique angle, and using a couple of hicks from the Midwest, I hope we can all consider the ways we treat people poorly... especially those that are not like us.

As always, thanks for reading, and tell a friend.
Cheers,
Ryan J. Pelton
February 2017

How to make an author crazy grateful

If you liked this book, and want to see more in the series, I can help. And, there are some things you can do that will help me out a ton:

(1) **Review this Book**

Go to wherever you purchased this title, and leave an honest review. You have no idea how that helps me keep writing and publishing. I want to build a rabid tribe of fans that want more of my stuff. Reviews are essential!

(2) **Become a VIP**

VIP's are what I call the people on my mailing list. They get latest updates on book releases, blog posts, and (best of all... wait for it) FREE GIVE-AWAYS!

Become a VIP today.

(3) **Get Next Book in Antique Assassin Series**

The adventures of Dexter and John continue in *Hired Gun (Book 1)*, *Stranger Danger (Book 2)*, *First Blood (Book 4- prequel)*. Dexter and John find themselves protecting LeClaire from crime families, family members, serial killers, and themselves. Find these titles where books are sold.

Thanks for your help, and thanks for reading!

Cheers,

Ryan J. Pelton

About the
Author

Ryan J. Pelton is a genre-hopping author with over seventeen fiction and nonfiction titles to date. He also hosts a popular writing and publishing podcast (TheProlificWriter.net). Ryan reads, writes, naps, dreams, and nurses a Diet Coke addiction with his wife and four children in Kansas City, Missouri. Email Ryan and say hello: RyanJPelton.com/fiction